SATANSKIN

James Havoc

"SATANSKIN"
by
James Havoc

ISBN 1 871592 10 0

First published in 1992 by
Creation Press
83 Clerkenwell Road, London EC1M 5RJ

Copyright © James Havoc 1991

All rights reserved

CONTENTS

SATANSKIN:

Satan's Skin.
Havoc.
Egg Cemetery.
Tropic of Scorpio.
The Venus Eye.
Devil's Gold.
Shadow Sickness.
Dogstar Pact.
The Tears Tree.
Succubus Blues.
Syphilis Unbound.
Ditchfinder.
Crimes against Pussycat.
Twin Stumps.
White Meat Fever.
Thirteen.
Tongue Cathedral.
The Colour Hell.
Demon's Spice.
Zodiac Breath.

Appendix:

RAISM - The Songs of Gilles de Rais.

Meathook Seed.
Moon Scar.
Magick Slit.

SATANSKIN

For

Alan McGee

SATAN'S SKIN

On a night like tonight, I can believe that this moment, this elliptic index in which all possibilty and impossibility merge, will never end. I can believe that the dawn will never come.

Reality is a neural raiment we shed beneath the counterpane of fast-dissolving daylight; reverting to our formative amnesia, we may live a thousand years as an insect or god in each allusive millisecond.

An illustrated gloom draws in. The norse, turbinal rain brings a succession of bestial faces; old, familiar glances, merely one flashing sequence in an unfathomable retinal spool of burnt-out frames. By an almost metastatic transference we once more attain the lodge of our infancy, that broken weft as untenable as the duration of an undercurrent dream; a wasteland of erupting graves reclaimed.

On a night like tonight, I believe that mud is nobler, more sexual, than flesh. It holds in its memory the upheavals of planetary birth, the very statutes of consciousness. The rocks, the trees, the shadows themselves are in collusion; every atom of every substance boasts its own irresistable force.

Tonight, they are begging to be loosed.

Lightning, hold my hand. Show me your face in black water.

Tonight, someone bad is wearing Satan's skin.

HAVOC

In the beginning, there was cocksucking evil. Then came Havoc.

Havoc rising, retromingent, flanked by her two excoriating hounds Leatherface and Teatcleaver, coated in vixen turmoil, fangs ranging at the sun. She had perfected the art of coagulating, becoming as petrified as the reflection of a goat in obsidian or, again, gushing like carious starlight over the spires of primitive, hymnal bone that sheltered mankind. Mastiff fodder. Their raving lips pulped the fruits of sin - Death with three depraved heads.

Remorseless, they poured in through meshed doors and windows, through hairline cracks in sanity and through the centuries; like an impulse, or a coiled curse flecked by the cinders of hope. Collared in high preacher metal, gorging at the ancient trough, her hounds. And Havoc, she-vampyre stalking an Earth illuminated only from below.

Pent sexual violence and mutilating thought wax eternal; yet polar zones contract, meridians are latticed together like dragnets. Time is a cycle during which all stars are exiled. Now, like tumbling dice, the harvesters have come to haunt my humble attic. Havoc, languishing amid blood and black dahlias; Leatherface and Teatcleaver baleful in their nest of mudlit femurs. And I alone must feed them.

I am the first keeper, and the last. Beyond these attic walls, superstition is moribund; without me, the hunters become the hunted. We persist. The hounds are content to lick and crunch fresh cadavers exhumed from the churchyard, or the occasional treat of abortion slops from hospital bins. But she - she thrives only on canned heat.

For months, I have brought Havoc adolescent playmates, boys and girls alike. She enchants them at once. I watch their fate through a grimy skylight: stripped nude and tethered to her strange bed with black leather thongs, eager, at first, for the lascivious torture to commence. For days, relentlessly, she preys upon them, arousing them with sickly caresses, tinglers of her long tongue, the whispered promise of obscene trysts; again and again to the brink of orgasm, yet never beyond. Mocking their screams for release, their hideously contorted bodies, she devours their boiling sexual ectoplasm. Soon enough, the victim's heart caves in. Mastiff fodder. I replenish the vampyre's catafalque.

Midsummer night.
The moon is in eclipse; the young have deserted the streets. Havoc is starving. Just for tonight, I must let her feed from me.

I go to her naked. The room resembles a perfumed slaughterhouse. Leatherface idly watches me, licking out a skull. Havoc is cramped in her resting-place; her eyes seem drugged, remote, like a reptile doll. She slowly rises, and bids me don the mask of a wolf. I fasten it about my head and lie back amongst the decay. No need for bondage; the keeper goes unfettered. Havoc disrobes.

Her skin is bluish white, and as she sits astride me the touch of it shocks like ice. Then I feel her tongue curl around and around my penis, which hardens at once, and at my arousal a warmth and colour starts to seep into her thighs. Through lupine sockets I can see her buttocks close to my face; her fingers, tipped with cherry nails, reach behind and pull apart these voluptuous cheeks, displaying the hole of her anus which has been heavily rouged. Seized at once by an epileptic desire to plunge my tongue deep inside this orifice, I dash aside the mask; just as my fingers clutch her hips, she shoots back a jet of scalding urine over my mouth, followed closely by gouts of a heavy liquid that stinks like old ambergris. I fall back, nearly choked, and Havoc turns to face me, steaming. A buzzing of trapped flies sounds behind her teeth. Her hounds begin to whine, shifting in the manger; the sound of my wayward heart completes this putrefied symphony.

In laying mortal hands on the predator, I have transgressed, broken unwritten laws; yet the fire of anal lust, a furnace in which we sacrifice the flowers of our repugnance, destroys all fear of damnation. I grasp her pubic mound. Instead of recoiling or striking out, Havoc seems transfixed by this violation, the termination of a centuries-old fascination. In that one instant, the maniac circles of her endless night puke their entrails across my psychic canvas: blood-filled lunar prints, tombstones plated with baby teeth that refract the abysmal solitude of the stars, lakes of hot meat stretching to the horizon where reapers and tragic archangels agitate golden vats of dung, flowers and tongues, winged skulls hovering luminously overhead, and wormy, poisonous hearts threaded on sea-serpents hung like funeral necklaces about eternity. Havoc is lost; we proceed in fugue.

Her shallow breath reeks like a grave for the living, yet the juices soaking her inner thighs have the attraction of nectar. I begin to stroke her swollen clitoris. The distressed hounds are up on their hind legs now, starting to bark and howl as they test their leashes. The heavy carpet of human debris stirs into life, mannekin-shaped excrements shrieking and dancing about the attic, bones exploding like firecrackers; the air dense with swirling, black rotten petals buffeted by nymphomaniac molecules. The catatonia returns to Havoc's eyes, colour and heat ebbing away from her flesh and into mine, a euphoric lesion, the rush of some pure, arcane narcotic. Craving the desolate ecstasy of the feast, I feel further along her labia, which are clotted with thick cold juice, until my finger finds her anus, lubricating its gaping rim. She sits back automatically, and the savagery of the hounds reaches a crescendo as I penetrate her frosted rectum. Havoc stiffens, impaled, like a stone carcass; the last of her energy suffuses me. I hear her final breath, an ancient noise like the knell from a fur chapel, and then the mastiffs crash from their tethers.

I await dismemberment. Yet the betrayed beasts fasten straight away onto the corpse of their mistress, Teatcleaver gobbling up the sweet fat from her breasts while Leatherface shears off her fleshy deathmask with foaming, millenial incisors. Abandoning madness to its last cannibal supper, I slam shut and forever bolt the door to that attic sarcophagus.

Come. Play with me.

EGG CEMETERY

Ashton's brain was mudsick, with a meat shack dead centre. A quintet of waxen underlords held him strung on venus loops, refracting his withered lusts through this pane of innards. For centuries he hung by his hair above vesuvial vats, eyes tossed, the furrows in his face opening and closing like the gnarls of a gallows tree raped nightly by some whoreless headsman.

Deep in the shack, visions of eggs coalesced. Ashton began to perceive a glory in his evolution, likening his thoughts to those surges of novane splendour that peel from the surface of the Sun, splashing irrevocably, the gaseous, red and shifting black turmoils of automimesis. Like a fecund rain he irrigated the planets, whipping soils into undulant mud, a protoplasm through which he could yelp his quintessential miseries. His other self hung in an egg, and from fissures in the eggshell came the most hideous chants; hymns to the abomination and annihilation of the female gender, hymns to the exaltation of pigs and porcine fornication, hot sties and slop-brimming troughs; hymns, above all, to the high holy Ovum - matrix of his insane justices and predilections, nucleus of the kingdom of Mud.

And thus did Ashton escape himself, becoming reborn - a brooding, psychopathic embryo in his egg all leprous and sunken in scalding mire, its vast interior sac noded with the stumps of sexual desire and other dismal fruits indigenous to that humid, bubonic delta. In the manner of all crushed kings deformed by the torque of time, his each and every thought turned to extinction and global prejudice.

The day of his coronation comes. No sooner is Ashton installed upon his cascading throne of sour silt than he launches a vile, malevolent crusade against womankind, projecting forth a conundrum of greedy little boys and things that came across Hell on a spider's web; knights of the oval dawn, lashing the She-race with a new kind of tentacle. They construct a spiralling garrison from carnage, a folly of pubic pelts and sawn scalps, the juice of exploded sexes, succulent stools speckled with tapeworms, spines rippled by the hand of rabies, crab-lice in patterns, nipples punctured by greedy flowers, all rigged tight with gelatinous hawsers of head integument and packed in ice. Insulated by his muddy cocoon, Ashton orchestrates genocide in perpetual, palatial winter.

From the ovary he conducts all manner of base atrocity, stamping his feet in joy as maidens are nailed to windmills, girls turned into garments, hags pumped full of pinecones, and widows forced to masturbate with the spike-ridden tibias of their disinterred spouses. While the frozen catacombs still resound with their torment, victims are immersed in clay, baked and glazed. These ornamental effigies are hung on cords throughout the land. Their ghosts cry out to the living.

Circe was a prostitute who heard voices. The butchering of her fellow women began to stir up inside her visions of a religious eroticism. One day, she just bundled up her bones and hacked out from the snake. No longer a slave to tongue pressure, she hung her men in strips and made them bleed, just as she was forced to at the whim of the wanton moon. By haemal telepathy, Circe was able to home in on auras of sexual violence. In her coat of peeled steeples, she repelled.

In bleakest December, her faith was rewarded by a holy vision: her mother, cooked and dangling from a deciduous gibbet. After this revelation, Circe travailed in barbed-wire sandals and sackcloth smeared with her own excrement, cut away to display her blossoming rectal stigmata.

Canonised by the brides of Ashton, she led them as an army, trailing the alluvial runt through pleasure-paved sewers, her passing commemorated by pyramids of male teeth. Her legend was depicted by runes traced in gibbet dust, boding the advent of a harridan in her chariot of boy-bones. Word came to Ashton. A piece-dog point back-driven, miraculous, was riding into the heart of the Egg on a frothy, scarlet surf of slivered penises.

The nightscape suffers many strange creatures. Ashton squirms around rocks in the mask of Mudboy, marking out with diamantine droppings the borders of his lands; haunting the cankered crossroads. As the crackling of testicular gauntlets announces Circe, Mudboy rises slow, a deathly Jack-in-the Box striping the loaded sky with his anamorphic pussywhip. The heavens close like a black book. Torrential fictions assail every inch of Circe's skin, latching limpet-tight to each hair, burrowing into abrasions. Bad creeds spring up in the shadow of her breasts, sheening her belly, and between her buttocks genocidal doctrines trample the soft flesh, tattooing a heavy manifesto of colonisation. Sentinels of biblical wrath appear, oscillating within a complex of topaz palpers; jewels shake haphazardly through an unclean lens. Ashton plucks an ocean from the pearl and Circe recoils with a bolus of electrified tissue between her legs, her womb discharging clots of matter in which terrified faces twist.

Ashton is preaching from the testaments of Mud, evoking eidolons of dirt from dormant streptococci just as wolf lies down with lambkin; twisting the whicker blade that sings of cross-legged Eros in a whaleskin barque, mirrored by mocking briny as he muses on mermaid clitoris and the machinations of telepathic prawns.

The piece-dog point back-driven sprays out geysers of hot man-offal, creating lagoons amid the dunes of some dream tropic whose inhabitants dwell in hives. They lay their eggs in Circe's brain and wait for Summer.

TROPIC OF SCORPIO

Shadow - feaster at premature burial!

In dreams, Julian saw morning as a goat, opaque and oriental, sunburst hooves steeped in human woes, storming in to devour the veil from his tulpa heaven. Molars crunched the jasper pall, dribbling topaz like a waterspout; nuggets from the high galaxy burning slow inside the sleeper's skull. Then, as laminas peeled away, showing a Deathshead on the seventh face of the dice, he would feel the abrasion of bestial hair, dragging him into light like a swimmer half-drowned in infected treacle pools that welled from the craters of ingrown antlers; bare feet slipping and sliding on a ramp of evil golden showers. Even on the cusp of the full moon of May, the Billy-beast came in curds, butting him into lucid desolation. Sick from vertigo, Julian staggered once more to the mirror. It was plumed in his pellet eyes - the beast must die!

That night, Julian slept in the garden, ringed with lacrimose violets, and dreamt of festival. He at head of table, and opposite, ten leagues yonder, his tulpa, old Nutcracker, faintly signalling through petal palisades like a ship lost to the very buttocks of the sea. All manner of fodder graces the gleaming expanse of mahogany between them; choice tangerines handsomely mounted in excised simian sphincters, huge vats of mind-bending porridge, mulled flagons of rabbit-drool, deep-fried wasps as big as milk-breasts, Babylonian beef, chine of python fritters piled into hives that sizzle with barbecued larvae, coriander pods stuffed with whippet-eyes, shuddering insectile custards; all set to frame the centrepiece, elevated on jade tiers: the birthday cake of bellicose, Saturnine scorpions.

Directly above, the full moon of May, pendent like a Christmas tree bauble, silver-blue cosmic spew bubbling from her star-graven nipplehead; the chilly, voluptuous curve of her lacunose rind almost within arm's reach, precipitating perpetual flower-storms. Julian, convulsed by laughter, declares to Nutcracker his avowed intent to cripple the wind with hammers, searching for enigmas on stilts and the colour of treason as he goes; wiping his brow with sheets of torn-out sky. The reason, he insists, is to better comprehend the squawking rags of a beggar's stump; to see in them the means to grow shit on trees. In turn Nutcracker, pants tugged down about his ankles as he braves an orchid vortex to sample each and every dish at table, proclaims his vocation to be the ensnaring of a ginger-haired rascal, whom he would promptly drive head-first into the fire-place in order to facilitate the stuffing of the wretch's pale-skinned arse with countless hard-boiled eggs. Cramming fodder into his mouth with one hand, with the other he mimes this perverse taxidermy, pausing only to polish his bloated belly as if it were some arabesque, pregnant lamp. Fired by the tulpa's fantasy, young Julian starts jacking off beneath the table, face fixed in an idiotic rictus, one eyelid half-closed. Nutcracker continues his bawdy antics, attempting to cork his own breech with a fat tangerine. The moon hangs.

All at once, Julian ejaculates over a swastika of hovering rose-heads; old Nutcracker's tangerine explodes out of his fundament and arcs towards a Venus fly-trap, propelled by the emergent head not of some genie, but of a slick grey tapeworm, uncooked and puling, peppered with retractile stingers; and, from the East, a derelict monsoon stabs in.

Next comes a razor-sharp crack of lightning; it brings to mind the splintering of some celestial paddock-gate. The luminous fall-out seems to linger. Julian feels himself drowning in ureic rain, semen, and burgeoning light. Nutcracker appears transparent. Defined only by the lengths of coprophagic worm still hooked in his colon, he quakes beneath a dining-chair as Billy-boy comes thundering across the foam-flecked sky, in gruff and bearded person.

Bucking and huffing, the dawn-bringer smashes his septic horns against the full moon of May, hooves threatening to stave in the festive table. With each blow, soft sparks fly out, not dying but multiplying, intensifying. Julian is prostrate, blinded, bound to night by a merest thread; sad Nutcracker disintegrating by the minute. Billy-boy backs off, readies for a massive charge. His split eyes radiate pure beacons of light as he rushes in and delivers the ignoble strike. The moon's crust peels asunder; then, like quicksilver, it coalesces again, immersing the goat's horns. Billy-boy rages, shaking his head from side to side, snorting and gnashing his teeth, yet try as he might, he cannot dislodge himself from the trap. His back hoof, kicking blindly, bursts open the birthday cake.

Mad, red, in deadly unison, the scorpions within teem forth and start to march in single file, claw to tail, towards their attacker. Clinging to the rank, matted hairs, they proceed up the stamping hind-legs; finally, one by one, they disappear up Billy-boy's backside. Soon the goat is bleating with pain as the invaders snip around his intestines, planting stings in veins and tender membranes. Some begin to gnaw his solar gonads, forging a new nest, while others emerge from the tip of his sparkling pizzle, cutting their way out like claw-bearing syphilides; filling their host with agony right down to the roots of his Billy-bones.

Eternity passes from cup to cup. The beast's lights are dwindling, dissipated by crawling agents of chaos and nightmare. The remorseless scorpions have started to hack through his alabaster underbelly, pincers ripping the skin as if it were silk. Julian relaxes at the first warm, dark splashes of blood; even the most brightly-halo'ed carry shadows in the soul. Huge clots pour down next, then the guts, and endless collars of steaming bowel; cloaking him in humid darkness.

Nothing left of Billy but a drawn, lacklustre hide extruding from the planet Queen.

The pine lid slammed shut, sounding briefly. Old Nutcracker toiled away, spreading layer upon layer of damp earth; with weary hands he tamped down the very last spadeful, sundering daylight and sleeper for all Time.

THE VENUS EYE

Coffinbound, Lovechild experienced the upper world by setting forth her left eye, Lucifer, on a supernatural leash. Prowling the local village and countryside, Lucifer would home in on sources of energy. Countless young lovers succumbed to his cyclopian inquisition; his favourite trip was the spiral down orgasmic spines. He could report the crackling voltage from a masturbating nun, then fly to embed himself in the hot arse of some farmgirl riding a jackanapes. At such times, Lovechild found Lucifer hard to control; senses overloaded by that unquenchable pupil, she would often have to struggle to retrieve her unrelenting spy. When she was finally back in blackness, the lid of her oblong box would suppurate with a mucal condensation, as if it were flesh and she the parasite within. Her face stank of lightning.

One sweet Autumn night, as Lucifer cruised the cobbled streets, hard beneath the gas-lamps so as to light his mistress' prison, he detected a prodigious incandescence emanating from one of the shuttered shops. At once he flew to its thatched roof, down through the rafters, and into the sparsely-furnished attic. It was instantly apparent that he had focussed upon a veritable furnace of lust. Shedward, the local butcher, was entertaining girls from the orphanage.

Lovechild beholds the scenario through Lucifer's anamorphic distortion. She can discern a ring of naked girls, none more than twelve or thirteen years of age, lying prone on the floor; seemingly enjoined in mutual cunnilingus. The butcher is squatting in the centre, clad only in his bloody apron, whooping and thrashing his own haunch with a riding-crop as he gleefully shits into a pail of giblets. Lucifer pans across the room. There, on an ebony rocking-horse, sits the queen of this pubescent coven. She wears a roasted rack of lamb for a tiara, and is veiled in raw suet and ligatures. Her nude body has been painted all over with animal blood. A girdle of hearts rests over her hips, pallid aortas skirting her pelvis, and rib-bones dangle from her small, pierced nipples.

The next second, Shedward is up behind her in the saddle, pushing her forward over the wooden mane as he lifts his apron and starts to wipe his foreskin along her perineum. The suet mask snags on the horse's ear and slides off. Although the face beneath is caked in crimson, and the transmission of its image warped, Lovechild knows at once the identity of this teenage meat-mistress.

Her daughter.

The vision curdles, dissolves in burnt amber. Lovechild starts to turn in the grave, over and over again, shrieking, railing at the lid of her coffin, nails striping the mouldering satin. She can think of nothing save the sight of her traumatized child, and revenge upon Shedward, the defiler; abandoning all concentration on her errant eye. Unbound, Lucifer plunges into the orgiastic fray; from orifice to soaking orifice he flies, into teats and brains and testes, sucking up electricity like an orbital sponge.

Unbridled power loops into Lovechild's torn psyche, sworded and scorpionic, pricking as if the inside of her refulgent cranium is being needled by a thousand nomad hornets. Her fontanelles dilate with converse litanies and tirades, pan-pipes feeding back into a primitive night illumined by shifting occult pyres, ritual murder and the blazing effigies of reaper kings; gold and scarlet swastikas surmount the moon. Archaic stars invoke phantoms, chaos irradiating torn-out hearts in carmine necromantic chalices, fetishes and glittering coils, ditches brimming with magma and silver faeces, haunted ruins shimmering under fiery spurting arteries of the sky; upward cataracts of dog honey in a valley of tongues that speak ecstasy.

Little Michaela was first to the window, pointing in awe towards the old graveyard. Following her wet finger, Shedward beheld what appeared to be a massive pyrotechnic display, or perhaps a fallen comet trail or conflagration of St.Elmo's fire, raging on the skyline. Spectral sparks endlessly criss-crossing a high, oscillating rampart of cosmic sulphur, while strips of mutinous energy lanced the atmosphere; tombstones, deep-sunken, like torched she-heads beneath this rainbow-hued inferno.

The butcher, a superstitious soul, often fancied he had seen faery lanterns dancing atop that hill. Loins piled high with lean steak, beady mind's eye pressed hard to a knot-hole in some mythic childhood fence, he would lie on the chopping-block imagining orgies of lesbian flower-dwellers: tiny, whip-cracking winged dominatrices in slugskin catsuits gyrating over graveslabs lit up by blazing petals, while eunuch elfin held aloft trophies of carious, grown-up molars; borne on a warm wind, slivers of sad, charred melody. Tears would flow from the butcher's eyes then, mingling with the cords of drool upon his ample chins, as he gently wept in the shadow of spinning, strung-up heifers shod in shiny vinyl boots.

Yet this firestorm, surely, was evidence of even greater forces; forces that Shedward was already longing to enslave. Abandoning his girls, he rushed to the street, shouting out to arouse the slumbering village. Soon, a confused mob had assembled outside church; some marvelling at the nocturnal lights, others fearful of evil magicks. Brandishing his cleaver like a holy sceptre, Shedward assumed command, proclaiming that they were about to harness the secret power of the woods; then, counter-armed with wands of vaulting ignition, they stormed the coruscating cemetery.

Cold flames turn their breath to lilac steam, fixed like pinned starlings in a maze of chattering, radioactive crosses. Far below, the earth begins to rumble. Shedward imagines She of Tombs, jacking off the dead. Soon their cold semen will kiss the heavens, dousing the mob's brands like a blizzard of angel teeth. The earth splits open. Lovechild has risen from the grave.

Shrouded in luminous ash, wailing like quicksilver, she levitates above Shedward. Black fireworks erupt from the pores of her smoking skin, fanned by the creeping beat of pinions greased with satanic butter. Shedward cowers down, voiding his bowels on a poppy wreath; Lovechild descends. They are face to face. Her right eye transfixes him with hate; left Lucifer is reeled in from girl heaven. He slips inside Shedward's mind, drinking in electrical impulses and pissing them back out into the void.

From Lovechild's empty eyesocket a speckled wardrum drops, followed by a goosetail and a dildo oozing hot, sooty phlegm; the manifest debris of the miserable butcher's persona. Ant-covered dials on cords tumble out, then pork-bone pariahs, a dog in a cow's orbit, eight-balls in egg-shells, clawdust, caves within kitty, figments from a chapel of flawed diamond skulls, two clockwork sailors, thunder on hooks, skin bells cut from the boiled slaves of birds, red honey in a head-cage, keyholes, hexed cobalt breasts, a dreamboat of rats, cups of puce tears beneath a tinsel tree, and a hymenopterous cupid caul with orchids; littering the boneyard like flaccid, discarded toys in a neon nursery.

Avenged, Lovechild lapsed into putrefaction. It was the end of Shedward; all his hair fell out, and he spoke only gibberish from that day on.

DEVIL'S GOLD

Gillespie awoke sweating excrement, face grooved like a silver bullet from a black gun. Midnight scars had filtered through the bars from the waxworks without, sinking scarlet stumps into the sleeper, tethering all dreamtime to Nemesis. Was there no end to this faecal conundrum? Gillespie had been splayed in a velvet hole for days, dogged by a moon rotting in its axis like a bad penny. Its every emission spelt immolation.

An anal pact is easily struck, but it leads into labyrinths whose demon is hard to beat. As instructed, Gillespie had hoarded his stools in a cauldron for thirteen lunar cycles, moulding each collection into an infantile effigy. Doubtless these mannekins were yet abroad, harvesting teeth of the sea and star-spittle, the sonic fragrance of death-rattles or livid paranoiac essences, talking eggs and a thousand other prizes to adorn the pit where the demon was coiled amid its primaeval gallery of skulls on spikes. And what of Gillespie? Raped in the cradle by a spectre of creeping whips, he had dwelt since adolescence beneath the soft hammer of an oneiric pathology; his reward, slowly realised, was the power to manifest the female animas that sluiced nightly through his psychic pans.

At first, he noticed only vestigial change; dilated nipples, fingernails that could rake through muscle. Soon he could alter the shape and colour of his eyes without cosmetics; he needed no blade to remove the hairs from his face - they dissolved with a wish. With each fetid baby delivered up to the demon, another shade of woman hooked into his flesh.

In dreams, Gillespie wanders sodden, hermaphrodite corridors, halls that resonate with the melancholy of outcast animal kings. He conjures forth and preens an eight-mouthed ululating penis, unleashes tulpas from the folds of his scrotum, drags cold reluctant somatic formations from occult slits. Cephalopods. He caresses his breasts on a throne of bones, while eunuchs swing in the void.

Now, when he wakes, memory persists. The dawn sky is frozen, heavy purple tallow, shot through with stars smeared like rectal kisses. Now, it will always be night.

At the thirteenth eclipse, Gillespie rose in the looking-glass. Suffused in perfumes and furs, she had infested the mantle of the moon as it hung nailed to its vitreous tract. Immersed in the lakes of her own eyes, she now understood why beasts screamed by night, why her emanations tore their souls apart. Raking her distended belly, imbued with the charge to blister blood and brine, she writhed in perpetual orgasm. Her tears were incandescent; she shone. In its lair, the demon also ejaculated.

Smouldering dark ectoplasm stained the house of Gillespie. A muttering doll of diarrhoea in flux spilled from its ditch and scampered away. But the demon, like most of its kind, was greedy and treacherous. The lunar bitch was gravid with madness, and could bear him many more offspring. This dream was cast in silver.

Henceforth Gillespie stalked in a furnace of broiling clitoral mesmerism, a brace of champing vaginas each side of her groin. More time-worn than the night, she lit up brothels like a holocaust and melted the wings of reality, flayed the face of sanity and used its skin for nightmare-leaking condoms. Countless men penetrated the trash inferno of her vulvas, perishing as the fangs within devoured their meat, lapped up their blood from the oval trough. Magic infants fucked each other in the hollow hides. Women too were drawn into Gillespie's web; for them, she would unfurl a phallus from her churning navel, injecting every orifice with hallucinogenic seeds, a legion of thirsting vampire bruises.

Spellbound by carnage, at first she scarcely noticed the faecal tinge to her perspiration as it wove its humid penumbra; yet soon the molten gutters were heaving with turgid waste, her cell soused in cataracts of excreta. Her holes would not seal over. She was halo'ed by the stench of latrines, crucified in the dusk - a nebulous church of plague larvae - while her lover lay masturbating in its crypt.

The demon had the segmented body of a worm. No limbs, just a long penis of reptile bone tipped with carcinogenic pincers, and a head of ossified manias. By the clicking of its scums Gillespie knew it, by its recidivism and simmering debauch. It was lodged beneath her hovel. Ravenous. When would the Sandman return?

He came with chains and a cacophony of razors, a swinging pumpkin lantern beneath his feral cloak, a plot of knives anchored in his gently rotting brain. His breath stank of semen and funerary ashes. Ah yes, he had the style of eternity, her lover; mummified wasps pierced his foreskin, graveworms sutured his veins. His black leather skin was corrupt with tumours, and his suppurating fingers bore bodkins that he plunged into her pearl-embedded pupils.

Living sickness wraiths her cot. Everywhere, predators. Phantoms of desiccated meat now throng her nocturnal craw, shrouded by a tortuous avalanche of cleavers. She wakes to escape revenge. The room boils. Walls throb with an arterial pulse. Auras of blood, venereal dementia, astral rape and deformity intermingle with the thrashing vitriol of excrements that bursts from her pores, bound to sate the demon underground. A glacial splintering heralds the jealous moon, reeling across its fractured wax heavens, lashing with caustic rays.

Gillespie's anus has metamorphosed into a third vagina. The only stools that slip from its scalding lips are bloodshot, and gallows-shaped. They shriek at the first bite of cold air. Two more vulvas yawn lazily across her armpits, foaming with fried chicken bones and cigarette stubs. Thirteen nipples ooze faecal lava.

That night her brood returns to guzzle at these stinking teats, crouching like incubi over her chained torso. Each dwarf swells as it feeds, until, completely engorged, it splits into several more creatures. Everything merges: walls, floor, bed, a single circus of pure excrement. Gillespie is a filthy, seething mass of clashing tides; one minute void of form, the next delineated as a nest of gargoyles. Finally unsexed, it perceives itself as an ulcer shifting in the rectum of some porcine deity. Suns and stars form a cathedral of maggots, where skeletons howl like flowers.

There is a stranger in the pigsty.

SHADOW SICKNESS

Even the skinless persist.

In holy houses you can hear the sacs bursting behind walls, blackness corrupted when flinty horns draw sparks across a chalice of guts. Anemonic castrati flit between cornices, dripping psalms; nuns huddle beneath the hides of those who haunt them. Their cells are cloyed with the smell of spent incense, mingling with a viscous pine-scent blown in from the nearby rookeries. Loveless, they endure the cold stasis of crayfish. Once little girls who skipped through sunlit rose arbours, they now weep in the shadow of abattoir mechanisms.

Sister Furgrave it was, who took up communion with the Jack of Hell. He appeared to her monthly, paying homage only during her menstrual period, drinking his fill before penetration. His skin had the texture of tarantulas, and stank like an ossuary. His tongue, long and ulcered with anuses, droning into her ear the obscenities which so unspeakably depraved her while his enormous, feathery penis carved away between her thighs. When he came, pints of freezing-cold semen flooded through her reproductive system - a supernatural sensation far beyond mere orgasm.

Yet the Jack exacted a high price for granting such favour. Even as he pleasured her, his goblins were abroad in the convent, claiming a victim whose skin they would peel off to add to their Master's collection.

The depredations continued into winter. Soon, the Sisters began to spy on each other. Sister Furgrave was observed in the wash-house; they knew her at once as a devil's doll, the portals of Hell incarnate, by the livid intermeshing talon-prints on her back; by her nipples, ragged and bitten through; and by the sight of her vulva, grotesquely enlarged like a screaming target.

In the heartless glare of the noon-day Sun they fell upon her, driving a thousand nails through her bones, then hanging the body from a flag-pole as a talisman against evil. The flayings ceased.

Midnight. Sister Crone, disturbed by creaking and scraping in the courtyard, presses her face to the bars. Sister Furgrave's corpse is swinging like a pendulum, grating on the ramparts. Cleaved to it, a hunched, dragon-winged shape, forked tail switching as its hindquarters pump in fornication. Lumps of putrefied pubis fall to the flagstones. Unseen cats begin to wail. The Jack of Satyrs has returned for his crucified concubine.

Fearing for her skin, Sister Crone hurries to the corridor. Everything is crusted in icicles. She returns to the window. Left of a bleeding orange constellation, the Hell-Knave is winging away forever with his bride.

Henceforth, the spirits of the dead know no rest. The convent becomes a theatre of apparitions; Sister Furgrave, hollow and amorphous, omniverous, and her glistening, raw-muscled coven, stalking the dormitories in search of epidermis.

Sister Crone, struck dumb and blinded by her encounter, is elected Saviour by the Sisters. They keep her tethered by the gates, half-naked, feeding her on crusts. Wayfarers, seeing the promise of copulation with a drooling, defenceless idiot, are lured to the convent. As they avail themselves of her trussed body, they are bludgeoned to death by the nuns and then fed through skinning machines. The salted hides are hung up to cure in the crypt. With each new offering, one more ghost is laid.

Finally, only the spectre of Sister Furgrave remains unappeased. The skeletons and guts of dead travellers afford her little satisfaction. She may not rest until she has retrieved her own, nail-ridden bones from Hell.

Hazel, the Exorcist, is summoned. He sets up his apparatus in the forbidden chamber where Sister Furgrave once gave herself to iniquity. Insisting that simpletons are closer to the spirits, he requires the assistance of Sister Crone in his rites. She is made nude, then tied to the poison cot. At once, Hazel sodomises her, proclaiming that a virgin may not act as a fit host for malevolence, which invariably uses the trademan's entrance. Then, without further ado, the ritual commences.

Surrounded by candles and diagrams, Hazel preaches from arcane bibles, peers into prisms, writhes around in drifts of pulverised offal. At the thirteenth hour, possession: Sister Crone, she who has no voice, starts to screech a blasphemous, profane litany. The scales fall from her eyes, which emanate the atrocious sadness of the disembodied dead; her flesh bristles with corroded nails. It is Sister Furgrave who now strains like a dog on the bloody bonds.

The nuns drag her, foaming and vomiting rust, from the charnel cell, and drive her with scourges into the wilderness, chaining the gates in her wake with finality.

One moment, the Jack of Hell is tangled up in lust with the meatless femurs, desiccated lard and fragrant, necrotic tendons of his beloved; the next, he is alone in his underground boudoir. His bellows of frustration and rage cause seismic waves across the countryside; the earth splits asunder, and the sanctified convent is engulfed forever within the belly of the Beast.

DOGSTAR PACT

Those with soft leather skin and fur entrails have little need of clothing.

In orgasm, Philbin envisaged metamorphosis as a mosaic of spasms, whose leitmotif was an inverted, slit cross of rancid meat. This system of mutant flesh was dominated by a white sun-face shooting bloody rays, dissolving as he ebbed into cataleptic sleep. These visions had begun with his wife's pregnancy.

As the months progressed, she could no longer tolerate sexual intercourse. Philbin expended his energies on the land. One evening, his raven-blue mastiff, Sodom, returned home from harvest with a dead dwarf clamped in its jaws. The prey was badly mutilated, neck bitten right through to the bone. Philbin was fascinated by the slick, glistering vertebrae on show; he cut out three of them, and carved them into dice. From the top of the dwarf's deformed oval skull he hewed a cup, and wiled away the long summer nights by casting his new tarot-cubes against the shithouse door.

On the eve of his daughter's birth, a whirlwind flared in the darkling haze of the North, inaugurating vertiginous insurrections against Nature. A netherworld pageant unfolded in rapid time. Mandragora sprouted from an unmarked grave; bees with human faces sprinkled pollen over the head of the slumbering Sodom. The dog collapsed into a violent, unstoppable bout of sneezing, its whole body convulsing, and died with dark blood foaming from its snout and penis. These tarns captured the image of the setting sun; in overwrought crepuscular arcades, cannibal scarecrows clashed. Ghost-drums hammered in the bleak cornfields. No matter how many times Philbin cast his dice, they turned up triple six.

A screaming breaks the spell; screaming that endures while Philbin runs across never-ending fields to the farmhouse. It ceases, finally, just as he vaults the porch. Wading through stacks of new green corn, manure-sacks and dog-chewed harebones, he bursts into the gloom of his wife's bedroom.

There is something wrong here. This should be a shrine of new life. A bright, joyous place.

It says so in the Bible.

But it is dark. So dark, and quiet. And it reeks not of life, but of death; something like an abattoir. There is even a carcass. A carcass that looks, in the wan light, ridiculously like his wife. Halved, lengthwise, from within.

Halting sharply, Philbin skids on her cooling innards; falling flat at the feet of his newly-born child.

She stands at least a yard tall on the bed, with black hair clotted in afterbirth down to her knees, the opaque eyes of a shark, and shining, coral-white skin. A length of steaming spinal cord is looped over one shoulder like a lariat. She is kneading her dead mother's dugs with both fists, gulping down the curdled cheese that comes squirting forth. In the flickering lamplight, her pelvis throws a canine shade. Between her open legs, glowering mutely scarlet, the cruciform vagina of the Beast.

Horrorstruck, Philbin is aware only of a swelling drum-beat without; then, the revving of chainsaws in the old barn, and a rising, high-pitched babble. With a feral grimace, Coral-White springs past him and is gone. Slipping in his wife's intestines, Philbin skates over to the window in time to see her vanish into the corn, flanked by a group of tiny, twisted saw-bearers.

Silence.

The world did not turn. Philbin sat on his porch, staring at the negative sky, for months. Or was it years? He could not tell, nor did he care. The mists of Time were fermenting, slowly, in his occluded soul. Still silence. Not a sound, save for the ceaseless clicking of the dice in his fist. No birds sang, not a single leaf grew on the tortured trees. The bleached, infertile soil was nothing more than a sarcophagus for the sun.

Finally, noise. The snapping of the brittle grey crops. Then the low sputter of motors ticking over, and gentle but off-key singing. The first deformed heads, swathed in nauseous ricks of hair, emerged from the fields. More followed, and on their shoulders Philbin could see borne a huge, symmetrical cross. Lashed tightly to its beams, a naked, pale-skinned girl with jet-black tresses.

Coral-White.

Older. Much taller. And unmistakeably, human. Philbin could see that her eyes, imploring him to reclaim her, were wide and limpid blue: her mother's eyes. He scanned her body. Although dark fur now covered her pubic region, it could not conceal the straight groove of her sex. Little caring by whatever magicks the stunted kidnappers had lifted her curse, he arose joyously to greet her. The procession ground to a halt.

A club-footed, chanting freak hobbled to the fore. The dwarfen king, nude save for a leather belt with pouches, his mad body all humpty and buttered with stumps, his scalp ejaculating wild ringlets of embalmed crabs. In his left hand, an oak wand. He flourished it once. The arid earth at his feet cracked open, grinning, and spat back the bones of old Sodom. They spun aloft, then formed a pentagram around him as they settled. His right hand beckoned Philbin into this arena, then fished around in the largest belt-pouch. There, nestling in his hairy palm, a trinity of dice honed from a widow's backbone. Philbin at once understood the troll's intent. They were to play for possession of poor Coral-White's soul.

For hours they fling their bones, the winning

and losing going back and forth. Dwarfs surround them, jeering and firing up their chainsaws when the king prevails, plunging into silent menace if Philbin regains the lead. The moon reaches its zenith; they stand even at the final throw. The dwarfen king casually flicks his wrist. The dice roll forth, and his minions erupt in a frenzy of gutteral cheering, saw-blades zig-zagging through the smoky night air. Seventeen. Philbin needs the maximum score to win, and it has yet eluded him.

Jiggling the dice in his skull-cup, he tries to imagine the certitude of insects. The way the wolverine sniffs out gristle. The magnetism of cobras, the unerring swoop of blood-drinking bats. He becomes entranced. The tarot-cubes launch themselves of their own volition.

Six. Six. And triple six.

Without ado, the dwarfen king rises to his feet, shrugging his buckled shoulders, turns and limps away into the corn that begat him. Glumly, his entourage follows suit.

Philbin is roused by a pathetic whining. He rushes over to Coral-White, ripping away the braided reeds that bind her to the cross. For an instant, he sees his anamorphic reflection in two soulless, shark-black mirrors, before the talons of the Beast tear off his face.

His winning dice twinkle, once, in the moonlight.

THE TEARS TREE

All around the Tears Tree, on top of a tumulus, Nightingale has excavated coprolites imprinted with codes of eternity.

Now, breaking them open like bread rolls, he sits and scours their fireless interiors, imagining worlds within each petrified genetic strand. Hot hair halls, walls respirating, pulsating with fist-sized anuses belonging to each and every species; blowing forth beasts of jurassic excrement studded with diamond-hard persimmon seeds. Old, meatless dead throb and glow with lacrimal vitality. He can feel the torrid, feculent air in his lungs, the nauseous sway of the undulant pelts underfoot. Reflected in the pupils of a shell-bearing weasel, his head resembles a black fur cactus, riddled with gaping red sores.

The transformer transformed.

A misanthrope since birth, when the delivering midwife proclaimed his left clavicle to display the contours of a shark-eating dahlia, Nightingale spent his boyhood years attempting to change himself into animal shapes. One day crouching and snuffling in a baffled badger's set, the next racing crabs sideways across silty river-beds, he spent endless summers in vain pursuit of this miraculous conversion. In the cool of night he would retreat to his favourite hideaway, an ancient tree nurtured on the blood and bones from a burial mound for mediaeval rapists. There, reposing on a crest of obliterated mica, rubbing his shins together like a cicada or lowing like a moonstruck cow, he began to formulate revenge on Nature; unable to reform, he vowed to become corruptor.

In later years, he progressed to collecting the droppings which he took to be the essence of each living creature. Bent on rearing new hybrids, he would perversely mould every sample into the form of another; sculpting rampant lion effigies from lizard dung, Siamese shrimp-twins out of ammoniac bat-cave deposits, ram-worms, feathered trout, and dozens of other mythic twists. Sustained by tree faith, Nightingale instigated a secret garden beneath the boughs, interring his soft, fragrant models in shallow nurseries. Thereafter, his lonesome midnights were passed in tending this miniature bestiary; splashing the soil with his watery adolescent seed as he spied upon foxes mating in the bracken.

Striving to promulgate this renegade zoology among his peers, he met with ridicule; he was also unlucky in love. Night after night he sought solace on the old unchanging hill, irrigating the tree and his buried creations with copious tears. Seasons came and went. One Spring evening, as he sobbed away, he became aware of a falsetto drone from above. He peered up into the shadowy branches; there, imprisoned in pendulous bright red fruits, were the yapping faces of every woman who had ever jilted him.

Physicians came; Nightingale was incarcerated with his mind in evil ruins.

Now, the asylums lie empty; the Tears Tree is once more blighted by the shadow of the mad gardener. Cross-legged, rocking, mesmerised by the parched ordure between his fingertips, surrounded by his unearthed treasure trove.

Fool's gold.

Down in the piping fur bowels of his bestial microverse, Nightingale is a rank outsider, a virus; the Anti-Tears risen to reclaim his bastard kingdom.

Thigh-deep in miscellaneous excreta, he is fast pursued by stinking, roaring monsters ridden by the broken-necked skeletons of garrotted sex-criminals; buffeted by careering microbes, elemental jellyfish hovering infernally throughout the recoiling labyrinth. Lurching into a caecum, he finds himself backed against a curtain of rotting belly-pelt. Tubers of filth clutch at his ankles. Even as the hunters bear down upon him, Nightingale feels a corporeal revolt. Fruculent faeces coursing in his chill veins, internal organs bedraggled with whiskers; a sensation of evolutionary glimpses, clawprints in desert magma under motionless, cinnabar starscapes consecrated to transmigration: the fleeting, headlong plunge from Supernature's convulsive parapet.

Finally, he achieves transformation, becoming a creature of pure rectal hair, pock-marked with open sphincters. A reedy whistle escapes from one dribbling red hole; hyper-spatial, anaesthetic: the scream of the Anti-Tears. Now Nightingale knows what it means to pass through the eye of the needle, to exist only in dismal reveries of the pleated and the worm-eaten; an abject aberration of jurassic evenings, disencoiled from all sense, an echo in his own compressed skull like extinct primaeval oceans heard in a beached conch. Photographed through a microscope, he might resemble a series of ectoplasmic faces on a spiral stairway, the ghost in a melted machine of his own devising; drowning stumps in a morass of fused desire. Denied the games of a doll, he has shrivelled to this: hatred.

His scream doubles; the hybrids in the first rank shatter. Yet their skeletal riders topple into the sewer with jerking pelvises, missiles of penile bone skewering the whining invader, holding him fast with cruel coccyx arrowheads. Gripped by saline violence, beasts, bone-men and bird-headed butchers fall upon him; the corridor swollen with the muffled sound of osseous talons raking dense matted innards, polymorphous hooves drubbing face-swathes.

Leper wings flutter in the sugar and straw.

The last keening of a ransacked head reverberates away; the casing of the Anti-Tears resides in a thousand fragments, whirling on ribbons of spectral gelatine about the Tears Tree as it sinks its roots ever further into the tumulus, sucking dry the grimly ranting bones, and thence into the very core of the carelessly turning Earth.

SUCCUBUS BLUES

Circumcised beneath inauspicious astral fallout, Rex spent his youth tormented by hordes of laughing skin; as desolate in his bewitched and bastard garret as an alabaster foal in a coal-black meadow.

Convinced his cicatrices would preclude human love, he began to forge company beneath the floorboards. Soon, seven concubines of pure sodium reposed underfoot. Easter came. Rex peered through his skylight, seeking, as ever, a benign horoscopy; he still saw nothing but sobbing galactic eczema. Treachery. Rex felt acculted, overwhelmed by a conspiracy originating from cipher. He knelt before the ikon of his father: a canonised anti-image within an ocean-pink corona, decademons crucified like rats in the sun. Scalpel-blades reared from the canvas; adulterous, sectarian, divining uneasy waters.

His supplications were met by a retort of nails and splinters, while skin bubbled across the walls and ceiling. Rex was aware only of the simultaneous advent of his recurrent demons: on his right shoulder, Edgar van Gavou, robed in rhapsody, shining with pristine ectoplasm; to the left, Ragvon Cadella with his cruel plumage and rawhide, filigreed in yammering yarn and torn-down hurly-burly. Cadella bullied like a brute angel, the rainbow of tongues that streamered from his ill craw urging Rex to strap on the spurs of vengeance. He spoke of treaties between the fanged and the fingerless, depicted paternal fiends cavorting in marriage bands of prepuce. Gavou demurred.

Shadows creased overhead. The mocking skin had lowered itself in night nooses, hauling the seven lovers from their exploded repository and dangling them in midair; for they had no wings. Rex peered up at the shifting row of crevices he had lovingly chiselled between each pair of hard white thighs. They appeared to be expanding, contracting, warping; finally becoming letter-shaped, spelling out *NEMESIS* in the fearful ozone.

The concept fell to the right lobe of his brain, embedding itself with an unknown velocity which seeks and gives no quarter. With feral breath he blasted the parasites from each shoulder. Ragvon Cadella hovered, leering across the room. Rex followed the red tracks of his gaze; Edgar van Gavou, the pacific, was spitted on an excoriating moonbeam loosed from the sad, milky arc of some sidereal crossbow. His eyes were little more than white slime. Pitilessly, Rex scooped him up and drowned him in a whisky bottle. His years of indecision were at an end.

Cadella had assumed a cubic fettle; his face was a kana for blood. Goitres opened and closed on his throat, signalling wordless proclamations. Drunken, Rex saw only the demon's vision of himself as avenger, captain of a gore-drenched slut pack. He felt a flock of soft hands upon him. His concubines, fully fleshed, fellonious.

It was the Easter of Easters.

Sloughed from an unnamed satellite of skin, the beast with eight backs is at large: Bloodboy Rex and his seven whores. Their purpose, their method, an incomprehensible puzzle whose windings attune uniquely to Bloodboy's caprice.

Each nightslide brings another consummation in the unbroken purple of their stifling, ileac honeymoon; another trophy culled and delivered to the altar. Surgeons, priests, parents of either sex; fists unclamped from sodium lips and manacled to cast-iron operating-tables. Bloodboy toils away without pause, performing ragas of resection and amputation, declaiming his sutural sonnets; the spoor of his needles and knives weaving an irreconcilable tapestry, a scar panoramic in which he sees vindication in rushes, impressions of a viscous period between wolf and dog. Society has misplaced one of its incarcerated gods; from a face inferno, fragmented sapphire discloses its stark thanage: in the very eye of a triangular storm, two young girls peel back the skin from their breast-bones. Inside, the night. A star vortex, airless, icy. Their ribs comprise the bars of a prison cell; there are people existing, breathing, inside granite blocks thick with lichen. A high window is paned with resin plates which refract the faces in the floor. Canines range from corner to corner, devouring each other's droppings, pads as cracked as old salt. Bloodgates strain behind cannibal satin.

Before long, the titbits and scraps of discarded flesh have grown into an immense, unbreachable monument, ringed in ravished cumulus, imprinting its horrible shadow across the Earth like four flies on grey velvet; a God-sized phallus that threatens to fecundate the Sun. Stranded at the tip of its colossal glans sits Ragvon Cadella, twittering; melting.

SYPHILIS UNBOUND

Foretelling the future by chancre configurations on his glans penis, Galpin was able to intercept information exchanges in the world of weeds.

A velvet-cropper in latex, princess elect of the nests, was riding her sunflower meridian: Zillah, oozing like the opium that clogged the rattles on her cockrel-claw cunt-keep; star-semen oiling a house of cancer. Galloping through portals of pensive beetle forceps came her fox-embryo outriders, flanked by surfer ants on gossamer discs that spun in opposition to the sun. Behind them, weasels hobbling under the burden of cardiac warts, fatted ticks in zombie flesh and ambulant shapes of sheer gonorrhoea; a storming, merciless troupe that drank in lifestuffs like wildfire, while Zillah hunted down her albino quarry.

Ahead lies Galpin, king for a day in a realm of capering plums, whey-face flapping like barleycorn drapes punched through the pectorals of glory. Crowned in cyclamen and trumpets of Dragon's Pizzle, hidden amongst fish-eyed wheat sheaves blessed by the miracle of atrocities, he fiddles with his mule-masked, mummified hagstones. They are as impotent as a noonday sun that dribbles after midnight.

Honey-puking hamadryads are sniffing his trail, stringing their lutes with the milky pubic hairs he sheds while masturbating to the Queen of Hounds and her stinking, prolapsed uterus; nearer and nearer, plucking notes that reverberate through his threat of ash and rowan. The greenfly on these twigs rub their smoking rear-legs in harmony. They sound like the clink and clicker of fornicating skeletons amplified across a pessary-strewn rift valley. Galpin wipes the sweat from his scrotum, feeds it to his Dalmation bitch. The hour of harvest is upon him.

In adolescence, Zillah had instigated a clitoris cult founded on a tenet of sympathy with animals. She believed that only in orgasm could humans attain that state of innocence, devoid of conscious thought, enjoyed by the beasts in the forest.

Naked save for boots and waist-length jackets of rubber, she and her cohorts would round up boys by night, shepherding them to the cemetery where they bid them dig up graves. Then, writhing split-thighed amid the wolfbane and cool, upturned humus, they allowed the thirsting youths to drink their fill at each orifice. Evicted corpses, stuffed with orchids, were hung like boudoir curtains on cords from overhead branches.

Flat on her back, dizzy at the kaleidoscopic stars, Zillah began to imagine sexual disease as a dark, sad wanderer in a valley of ravens; the truth-bringer ever travelling under malediction. An undead spy, lean and devouring, dormant in ransacked atomic chambers, revelling only in the body's nether spasms, the upsurge of its most deep-seated wellsprings. Then conjoining, like the prodigal returned, drawing all extraneous energies to sacrifice in his unfathomable nucleus; glorifying the transience of flesh through a decadent mirror.

Soon, Zillah would only court the attention of much older males, men who might harbour the predatory paramour she longed to embrace. No longer welcome in society, reviled even by her sisters, she herself became vagrant, her errant figure staining the world just as she hoped an erogenous voyager would one day haunt her interior landscapes.

And so Zillah set forth in search of stricken flesh, attended by a caravan of weird fauna. Nailing choice morsels to the slab of obsidian which she bore across her shoulders, she began to construct a mirror of her very own; a glass in which her all-consuming prince would one day come to light.

On, Zillah, on; scythe poised to reap albino meat, and the clairvoyant sores that circle it! On, until the clucking of your frog-winged vanguard sounds its alarum at the fugitive's first wall of defence: the She-hound. Curling jowls bearded with jackrabbit thews, Galpin's familiar crouches defiantly on the bridlepath. Zillah can see that the dog is a shape-shitter; its straining, bullseye-dappled haunches are giving vent to irregular septagons and triangles, which in turn emanate turquoise ghosts. Preposterous visions compose their wall of weeping sleep: saurian sacs that pustulate in the forked tail of the whirlwind, anacondas gleaning honey from a priest-head cluster, a cabinet of dead jackdaws in the rain. Deathshead moths have alighted on the bitch's teats, which hang in morose rows, pitted by Galpin's milk-teeth. Its howls breach a sky of orange rags.

Only Zillah stands unrepulsed by this display; comprehending the signal novae in a dog's orbit, she is able to communicate a beautiful, viral spectre of her own: the apparition of hydrophobia. Senses scrambled, the bitch bolts, foaming with blind fear. The chimeras from its faecal polygons dwindle. Beyond the vaporised wall cowers a sweating fugitive, pasty chops puffing like bellows. His face resembles a cantaloupe of rotten ham, all awry with deliquescent chalk. Galpin whimpers as the huntress stands astride him, urinating onto his face; then, without resistance, he submits to the glittering blade.

Abandoning her victim, Zillah affixes her latest prize to the mirror of contagion, at last completing its putrid frame. The inky stone begins to clarify, images coalescing in its sorrowful, precarious depths.

Images of destiny.

Through the decaying funnel of pirated, prophetic abscesses, Zillah beholds her wedding day. She in a hooded gown of red velvet, vivid carnations wreathing her brow - clashing with the green, mortified tissue beneath, the fused features of tertiary necrosis. On her warped arm, the groom. Her saturnine avatar of carnal decay.

Yet he appears different, somehow, to the virulent knight in her dreams. White. Far too white. And flabby. Ugly, sweaty, ungainly. Snowy-haired, and pink-eyed.

And emasculated by her own fair hand.

DITCHFINDER

Alas, poor Gutrig! - The very cunt of night has bled into his sleeping mouth.

Star-saturated, he was spewed up and carved down in a hole where bad things shed skins. His Daddy would come home from killing drunk on arterial mink blood, fisted with reels of gleaming viscera, sulphuric vomit fonting from his copper-graven gizzard. He had four testicles; barbed white worms poked from the abscesses on his huge, unclothed penis. While Gutrig gorged on regurgitated meat, he would root around inside Mummy. One night, his fearful rummaging split her in two. Down amongst the compost and cockroaches, Daddy howled and howled. Gutrig looked up at the grievous vermillion sky. It resembled a face destroyed by sharp teeth. First came floating organisms, like ciphers for destruction, and beyond them the planets, dancing with the elgance of burning children. Under this bad zodiac, he abandoned the nest.

Alone, a sad scavenger in the rank, unbounded wilderness. Thorn-riddled hearts dangle from the vicious trees, whose fruits bear the seeds of cannibalism. Everywhere, open graves. Gutrig comes to a place where no dogs howl. Here, the heavens are negated by the copulating cedars, and the only illumination drips from overhanging gargoyle-lanterns of oppressive iron. The serpentine path is demarcated by piles of stripped skulls with pizzles rotting in their eyesockets. At its end, he spies an edifice shaped and shaded like a bruised mouth: the palace of the Queen of Slits.

She is caparisoned in a grey, wriggling cloak of

live rats, stitched together with catgut. All manner of knuckles adorn her brow. She parts the cloak. Her skin is fathomless and mercurial, an elastic mirror in which Gutrig catches the first ever glimpse of his own face: a smudged portrait, the semi-digested flesh almost molten over glints of bone; no nose, just a spike-filled maw and the solitary eye, adrift beneath a clouded yellow cataract. Startled by himself, Gutrig fails to notice the Queen's soft approach until his senses are assailed by a fish-head stench. Tracing its origin, he comes face to face with her fabulous genitalia.

Loaded like iron, Gutrig is slowly drained of all consciousness by means of a sexual lesion; dimly aware only of the arhythmic whirring of her lethal reproductive organs from beneath their adipose dewlap of stubbled, greasy skin. On a brink, he senses the advent of some massive universe; the very seams of fear are about to burst, and a delinquent aristocracy shall pray before the crimson altar.

There are ditches within ditches. The Queen's elongated labia snarl corruptly, disclosing the suggestion of a twilit, carniverous poppyfield. Gutrig can soon discern this interior domain with intense clarity; its iconic, ruby dawn, filtered through a skin-chilling mist, meaty and sugared, pervades.

Everywhere, wheels bearing gutted torsos that teem with web-dwellers. Ahead, the caves. Here Gutrig found Daddy, the stone walls of his home daubed with friezes depicting life in the belly of a raven. Flat on her silvery back amongst a tangle of pelts, legs parted, the Queen. Her dismal cloaca gapes open, bloodied and sperm-sprayed, a frayed orchid. The orchid starts to whirl like a dream-grinding machine, Daddy kneeling before it, shaking, and Gutrig suffers the impression of watching locusts in combat behind stained glass.

At a masque inside a girl where billy-goats gnaw salted feet on sticks and magpies pick at the gangrenous wounds of gold boys fallen from the sky, father and son swing on cords. Pods open and close, revealing fat rows of puce male organs; the Queen is on her rat-fur throne.

Proudly, she holds aloft her orb, a vase of bone-stripping acid, and her sceptre, a slender pair of corroded castrating tongs. Soon, these religious tools may terminate Gutrig's journey to the end of the ditch.

Yet the stalking grey skeletons that mock him can can only mimic her music-box tempo; as it winds down, their parched limbs stiffen. Daddy is a hunter, versed in the joys of snapping prey - even the bloodless provide, spurting hot marrow across his jowls. The Queen reclines in her seat, pulling her thighs apart like a contortionist. From her vulva, a circle emission of glowering narcoleptic rays, glutinous rings of hypnoses and concentric trances. Her eyes promise ritual murder. Gutrig's last glimpse of Daddy fades, and he slips once more into the vortex.

Voices. As raw as an angel's liver pecked out by vultures. Hooded ones are holding Mass in their hidden jade temple. Gutrig hangs by the neck over a gore crucible, kicking and convulsing, spurting moribund universes. Before his eyes, cascading religious signs, seemingly hacked from hemispheres of gristle. Scimitars appear. Then the hemp snaps, plunging him into a gaugeless, sardonic deep.

Dankness. Claws across his cold face. His grave is shallow, a brackish rattery by a dead river. The air is gloomy, heavy with excrement. Through this dreary, tainted tract, he carries home to Daddy an image of the Queen, encased in a bead of bilgewater.

Where is Daddy?

A distortion of smouldering black musculature, he appears through a succession of oneiric mirrors out of time. The seventh and final mirror, convex and scorched, is the taut back of the Queen as he fucks her like a beast. One hand squeezes together her breasts, while with the other he twists and tugs a coarse noose which is knotted around her bruised, bloody throat. Listening to their whining and growling, Gutrig suddenly feels an immense pressure on his ribcage, forcing the air from his lungs. On the point of asphyxiation, he sees himself blasted from a sow's backside.

Sprawled across his familiar bed of carapaces, husks and nettles, he watches as Daddy, roaring with laughter, butchers the sow and proceeds to roast her up for supper. For Gutrig, the shivering brains. Sweet woodsmoke curls to the pink and benevolent sky, while a reassuring warmth permeates their home. What could ever disrupt their newly-regained harmony?

With a contented yawn, his regal step-mother uncrosses her legs.

CRIMES AGAINST PUSSYCAT

The Sphinx - loneliness as a cold altar.
Fellating kittens in a witch-house, Momus began to hear the chime of ancestral voices. Soon, spoilers came from the dark side, playing panther-music on his sternum as he slumbered.
One night he awoke, dry-mouthed, from a nightscape soaked in tails. Throughout his quarters, an eddying groundswell of numinous, psychotropic illumination. At the foot of his bed he could discern the form of a large he-creature, black-skinned, cat-headed, covered with strings of pigeon skulls. Its breath stank of apples and oysters. A pearly set of claws flourished twice, leaving snuffed-out photon trails that hung briefly like an odd crimson rune, the crock of iniquities at rainbow's end. Then all light vanished without flicker, reminding Momus of that moment when the noose snaps tight about a young murderess' throat. In a trice he was asleep once more. He slept profoundly, for hours on end, his nocturnal canvas now scored with caricatures of genital mutilation and other cackling anathemas.
Nothing stirred in the witch-house.

Morning. Seven storeys below, Lupercalia sits and greases the tools of her trade. Long since bored with her given lot of pumping slack gash in dirty basements, she is now fired by wild and daring ambition. Whilst servicing two novitiates with spring-loaded dildos, she has managed to decipher from their delirious babble the kernel of a long-hidden truth: the truth about Momus. This mystic runt is, it seems, the offspring of some blasphemous miscegenation: progeny of pussycat and preacherman, he is the last in an ancient line of familiars, the apogee of occult learning given human shape. Now, Lupercalia plans to taste that learning, to rise above her prurient mistresses.

Singing songs of whipcord, she sets off to work. Slattern-hounded, happy, sad, bent on terminal penetration; loving her ladies till they rot.

Feeding from a taurus lode, the young hags are already aroused; preening in bull-pizzle wraps, lewdly reclining on planquins of horn. Lupercalia opens up her scuffed medical case and selects the two most impressive instruments. With vigorous application, she soon produces a state of ecstasy in her patients. She listens intently as their talk turns, as ever, to the dweller in the attic; in particular, to lascivious speculation over the nature of his sexual organs. Lupercalia knows that the witches have never mated Momus, never sought to propagate his magick potency. Why then did they not have him castrated, as was their wont with the poor Toms that lurked in the scullery?

That night, on a mission to seduce and slice, she determines to resolve the mystery.

With a purloined key she infiltrates the cloister, choking on the stench of excrement, dried cat-piss and regurgitated herring. Clasping a scented rag to her lips, she searches out her quarry. Momus is perched on his bed, rocking back and forth, silent. At the sight of female he becomes instantly excited, pulling out for display his pride and joy: a massive, heavy penis the colour of over-ripe loganberries. Smiling, Lupercalia reaches down to stroke this unnatural organ. As Momus lies back, with a terrible purring sound like phlegm from an anus, she changes to her left hand; deftly slitting his member from root to tip with a hidden razor. While the catman shivers in shock, she tugs away at the opened skin. It starts to unfurl like a scroll, finally hanging to the floor on red threads from the scoundrel's original penis, now revealed to be no bigger than a baby's forefinger. Shaken by indelible delight,

Lupercalia rips away the fleshy sheet, flees the squalid quarters, and locks herself away in the basement with her bloody prize.

A grid of glyphs is tattooed within this roll of priapic fat: an entire malefic alphabet, the sum arcane knowledge of centuries. Spells that can incur death, undeath, or life in a vinegar jar; spells that can strip the skin from a ploughboy and march it to the nearest keyhole; set clothes-pegs on a rampage or turn bonfires into gripe-water. Spells that can cook a redbreast in suet on the wing, drape oceans across the saddle of a rocking-horse, place vertigo in the dreams of volcanoes; spells that can bury a demon, or raise one.

Spells that can liberate Lupercalia.

For days she practised, trying out chant after chant, rubbing herself raw with the inducing of more efficacious orgasms; at last, her chosen one came forth. He came with the scree of arctic arenas, a harbinger of tears, progenitor of ordeals. An obese Incubus with jet black ice beneath his foreskin. By night he settled on each witch in turn, fucking them as they dreamt white dreams. Soon they were frozen, turned into icicles that slid from the bed and splintered into a thousand shards across the limestone tiles.

All the while, Momus hissed and caterwauled and spat in his cloister. Scratching at the scabs on his penis, he eventually split them, releasing malignant jaguar sprites which, at first incorporeal, soon took form from puddles of diarrhoea and octopus. Desperate to regain the scroll before every witch was reduced to frosted smithereens, these fluctuating shapes seeped beneath the door and then flew at the Incubus as he fornicated, lodging themselves between his buttocks and pecking at his exposed membrane with deceased, undersea beaks. Irritated, the Incubus sat back heavily on the floor, crushing his persecutors. He got up, flab undulating, and slowly hauled his bulk to the attic.

Momus was propped up on his bed; barely alive, surrounded by foul haemorrhages. A pair of sprites were rolling around weakly in one corner of the room, trying to coat themselves with fish scales. The Incubus trod on them. Then he snapped off his left forefinger and held it against Momus' throat with the bereft hand, while his right changed into a mallet of solid meat. One blow nailed the catman to the wall; a breath of boreal flame set fire to his squirming body.

Even as Momus burned - and he burned in the cold fire for several long days - the Incubus installed himself as king of the witch-house, with Lupercalia as his Queen; announcing his intent to usher in a lustrum of sodomistic rape. While his attentions turned to the preparation of their marriage bed, Lupercalia unpacked the magick skin, seeking an inscription to rescind his advent - in vain. She had neglected to salt the hide, and it was already little more than a tray of larvae.

Lupercalia had jumped from frying-pan to fire; indeed, the smell of roasting flesh hung in her nostrils until the day she died.

TWIN STUMPS

Silence - sweet harbinger of disfigurement!
The family must die, but without the family there can be no sacred crimes. How mundane it is to kill or rape a mere stranger - masturbation by a ringless hand. Henry sinks his rigid kin into frosty meat pits, an ancestral burial womb insulated with sleek maternal pelts. When the full moon rises, he and the lonely dead come out to play.

Henry, last of the bloodline, presides in this organic mausoleum, where a clock driven by thorny hearts records thirteen fathoms of midnight. All the furnishings are styled from the dead. The exterior walls are proofed in human skin, tattooed with pornographic tableaux, and the roof is cobbled with eyeballs so that all the pretty stars have mirrors.

Inside, the family are at table. At the head sits Henry, and opposite him his exalted brother Griezell, a gothic foetus on nails. On either side, four generations. Mummified, necklaced in teeth and testicles, pierced all over with tarsals; some skinned at death, others at birth. Half-eaten, bladdery and bloodless, some barnacled with transplanted nipples, some sporting multiple genitalia, legs screwed into arm sockets or heads crammed inside gutted bellies. Carpal chains leak from desiccated fundaments, rare maggots squirm in brain pans and pubic wigs.

As an adolescent, Henry had visions. Gazing up nightly at the steamy firmament, he came to realise that each star above was immaculate, a perfect and uncompromised entity. Evolving from dust, and later reverting to nuclear ash, the stars had no need to marry or multiply, no need to align themselves to familial groups. Astrology was akin to vampirism; constellations arbitrary, an atavistic conceit of man.

Filthy, uncomprehending man. Groping in misery; forever reproducing in the vain hope of burying his unutterable solitude in numbers. Slowly, his profane inter-breeding was dissipating the irradiance of his autonomous stellar analogues. Soon, the heavens would be extinguished. Henry could see but one solution: a glorious extermination of the human family.

Mocking the antics of his parents, he took to fornicating with the sows in the barn. Some grew gravid. One night a storm came, and the sows dispersed in terror, leaving behind their stillborn farrows. In the fulminating light, the tiny corpses seemed to Henry half-human. Heeding this omen, he took up the hatchet. Parents, brothers, sisters, aunts and uncles, sons and daughters alike were systematically axed and buggered, partially devoured and then preserved in subterranean vaults. The swampland acquiesced gleefully, guarding the scene of the crime with a rampart of grasses, prickling nettles and vines, quicksands and the mauve whorls of its erotic trees, whilst providing a fodder of dwarf hogs, mambas, and hot, horny fruits.

Every full moon, Henry re-enacts his violations.

Tonight, there must be a trial. Henry has reason to believe that Uncle Nexus, spurred by renegade shafts of sunlight, has slithered in his tomb and committed acts upon Mother, impregnating her with lobster claws and the jawbone of an ass. Soon, she may give birth to reeking shells or albino centaurs, crippled with eyes of syphilis resin; venomous usurpers in the mortuary.

Henry brings order with three sharp raps of his shinbone gavil. He turns to address the jury, thirteen puppets of addled blubber roped in a spinal gallery. Just then, the skies occlude with an inflorescence of whippoorwills; a lilting, disembodied voice interrupts proceedings, soiling the chapter of his law.

It comes from without. Pale Henry quits the chamber to locate its source. In his head, a mess of sick talons, itching; his breath like a premature burial. Trembling, he is lured into the gloom by a nursery lament, its chasmal sadness spelling the assassination of liberty. A girl child is sitting cross-legged in front of a skull-ringed acacia, scraping shit from her shoes as she sings; a stain on her panties recalling the genesis of comets. Confusion. This girl is not of the family. What possible fun then in stringing her up, whether it be to butcher or sodomise? Yet here she is, fresh from the marsh, an outsider in the gnarls.

She has a sticky doll with her, a tar baby dappled with hornets and dragonflies, and she calls it Miss Leopard. Miss Leopard has guided them through the swamp; now she tugs her companion to her feet. The two visitors start to skip in circles, widdershins, the little girl singing a heart-rending ode to ravens. Entranced, Henry flings himself to the ground, face pressed close to the rank loam, contorted as if licking dog-meat from a soft trap. His exterminating angel has descended.

Snakes pass. Girl and tar baby veer off into the swamp. Henry hurries after, powerless to combat his inexplicable attraction to the intruder; his every fibre ablaze with an insurgent desire to maim, to crush, to crucify.

Ablaze with love.

Deeper and deeper into the humid vegetation he pursues them, through vast spider-webs decorated with mortal remains, pools of iridescent vermin, leeches on the wing. Too late, he realises they have entered the quicksands.

Their trail is obscure. Henry hesitates. On the point of turning back, he sees the girl appear across a tarn, waving her panties like voodoo. Sure of his attention, she hitches up her dress, legs apart, giggling as she displays her hairless loins, tattooed with pig skulls, before skittering off. With a bellow of lust Henry lurches after her, mindful only of a crimson slit amid the ink-bones; yearning to snap the pinions of desire between his ceremonial fingers. His thoughts are sparks vaulting through the blackest pit. Within his soul, the geometry of molten lard.

In a trice, the thirsty sands envelop him.

The girl reappears. She raises her skirts again, this time twisting to display her small buttocks. There, at the root of her spine, hangs a stubby, curled pink tail. She defaecates loudly, her excreta resembling clusters of steaming raisins, then kicks off her shoes, aiming at the drowning man's head, to reveal a pair of ragged trotters. With that, she vanishes, giggling, hand in hand with tar baby. Spewing grit and slime, Henry perceives that his teenage nebula has regrouped; a spectre of high holy incest is once more roosting in the mangroves.

The moon wanes. From the vitrified sky, winter photons that kiss with thin cyanose lips, charged with universal melancholy. The swamp folds in on itself; the quicksands swallow the last of Henry. In his crypt, the family still sits, motionless, at the mercy of the disintegrating dawn. Their last living descendant is playing with Miss Leopard among the flytraps.

WHITE MEAT FEVER

The moon commands the torrents of creation. Yet so too does the body of woman.

Hatched under a lunar bane, Turner grew up amid dark sexless days, id nurtured in a conclave of retarded asteroids. Vowing revenge on the cosmos, he pursued sinister paths until one day his demon occurred in a brimstone mirror. In return for the sacrifice of his hair, Turner was granted the utterance that steals. He began to harness She-power.

Rose had always loved the night. She viewed its pall as malign tar, shot through with living dolls like a coven of claws, a canopy that could consummate a thousand curses. Scorpio vanes conducted her sex energy into webs. On Halloween her victim came already naked, all hairless, pale skin glistening with an unguent of oyster grease and cinnamon. Numbed by lascivious scents, with eyes fixed on her crotch - an arrangement in black and gold displayed by her raised skirt - Turner shambled after siren; he followed her to her dungeon, mesmerised by the bare, swinging buttocks before him, each emblazoned with a tattoo of peach-stones. Now it was Turner's time to pray.

Stitched into a suit of civet hide, with a Roman candle jutting from his fundament, bound to the nitrous rock by a concatenation of tiny petrified wings; Rose prostrate before him with split thighs and religion. Strangling on his secret garden leash, Turner's face is close enough to see the pearls of sweat on her pubis, to inhale her bizarre odours of strawberry lemur oil and runic rust; yet his tongue falls short of the ditch. She sings a loop of syllables he is condemned to repeat - his voice waxes heavy as a tombstone and resonates as if devils are casting knuckles for his dying soul.

Dawn approaches.

At the last, Rose unlinks her victim. Like a wad of offal from a car crash, Turner is upon her, snuffling and choking with snot, his furious penis slipping around her groin, the veins on the hairless scalp above her face bulging out to spell *Mother*. Suddenly, ecdysis: she sees his pupils dilate and flood outwards, until the entire surface of each eye is a shiny black screen upon which plays an ancient film of slaughter. Foul, protozoic words slither from his lips, the epitome of plague. As he comes, gibbering like a crippled mastiff, Rose is plunged into a comatose sleep. She will awaken to a Hell of sex-forsaken sorrows.

In his hovel, Turner leers naked before a looking-glass. There, between his nipples, is a chattering and braying vulva, its ring of hairs plaited with golden bows. He smears its juices over his bald pate, reflecting joyously on the origins of belief.

A weird maelstrom of winter comes. With it, a strange new chastity amongst women - the Cunt Thief is abroad. Yet, by the Solstice, Turner's labial larceny is complete. Mewling vaginas entrench every surface of his body. Like pets, he has named each one after its donor; proudly he whispers to them, strokes them as he feeds them gobbets of fried chicken, eggs or walnuts. His favourite, Lydia, runs across the palm of his left hand. She hisses and pukes fish-bones.

On the shortest day, Turner serenades his slits while baptising them with sweet red honey; he then sets forth to usurp the catamenial throne.

True faith is found on the altar of clitoral psychosis. Bristling with fallopian magnetism, Turner haunts woodland and misty glade. Streams boil as he passes, she-creatures ovulate and moan. Henceforth, he alone will revel in the empires of the Sun, debauching the velocity of living and dying, monarch gland in the brain of creation. Harsher than gold, the ribs within his pulp of magick slits form the spokes of a giant galactic wheel careering through inner space; while two hundred glistening lips whisper sedition, the millenium of Turner will commence with a solar orgasm to finally annihilate the tyranny of the dark.

Alas, the prescient moon has fled her heaven! Turner is truly alone. He shivers in the grave unlight, so silent he can hear scorpions mating. Mocking insects dart from mushrooms of drugged silk, hatchlings lounging on bales of teat fur pelt him with parabolas of frigid phosphorescent oil. In their green flash he sees the rotting dead, coerced from the Pit by pucks of sour vomit. Vampire bats rain excrement upon him. Swarms of mantis spermwing, crystal feverclaw, all those who deny the dawn, conspiring to spellbind Turner. Even the trees attack, tumescent with diabolic adrenalin, and beyond their homicidal canopy a pitch ocean crashes shoreward. Great scavenger gulls wheel in from the East, talons dripping bilious carrion while, far below, the depths are commanded by enormous white sharks, versed in mysteries that man will never glimpse.

Turner teeters, poised on the cusp of a sidewinding venus. Ditch cancer. In the absolute, atrocious darkness, he sees his own soul mirrored. Hollow, menopausal. His vaginas are growing parched and shrivelled, as arid as his dreams. Then comes a lightning bolt, and artificial sunspots flare cruelly on his retinas. Ululations and tendrils taunt his blindness; cuntless vegetable girls drop from the boughs above, dancing on ghostly nooses as they join in the invocation of the night for its sister moon.

The moon responds.

From a tarn she looses sway, inducing a final, mass menstruation in the body of the imposter. With a sigh Turner falls, lifesblood gushing from a hundred vulvas, blue flesh hardening like sheet metal. The storm doubles in, ritualising the sky which appears like the marbled haunch of some defaecating goddess. Lightning blasts an oak. Galvanised, its erect branches swoop down and fly deep into every one of Turner's clotted orifices, fucking him to the core, hoisting him shrieking into the air, body shaking and ripping up like pack-prey. He finally flies apart, pelting the far terrain in a sultry crimson hail; echoed at once by demonic cackling from a luxurious satellite of hair.

THIRTEEN

Beasts and dolls alike suit chains. Rooted in the soul, beneath tragic mind-blossoms, broods a longing for delusion - witchcraft.

The city is shaped like a hypnotic pattern. West of a hovel, dawn is delivered prematurely, a shrieking embryo of clotted amethyst. Steeped in its carnal hues, Quinn reflects upon the measure of his kingdom. Sadly, he finds it lacking. For what is a king without his queen?

He unsticks the bloody sheet from his back, letting it fall across the snub of his penis. His belly is scored like a side of pork for roasting. A crimson whip-trail from bed to door, all that remains of Miss Anastasia.

She is the one he warned her of, slit-bearer with a heart of thorns, and he is the sacrificial swine. Shackled to the sty, wallowing in the tatters of sexual pacts anulled by the dawn, he relives the queasy thrill as his limbs were first pulled taut across her septic gash anvil, senses brutalized by sensual hammers, the day she lapped up his shadow like a dog from Hell.

Quinn slept on rubber sheets, held rites of cruising the backstreets, licking used contraceptives. Shuffling through snow in a tiny suit, dreaming of young girls and their flagellated buttocks. Looking for perfect traces. Each midnight, he craved the intangible like a thing unchained.

It was the coldest of winters, the pinnacle of romance. The domain of a moon with boils upon its crescent rim. On a crackling and leprous evening. Old Quinn - alone. This time, something bristled in the air. Fleshy, oceanic. Movement like brains clinging to walls, glimpsed through a crystal entropy; dashing the virgin eye to flinders. The night, frigid and godless, whipped upon him like a bloodsucker made of two girls. In the shitpool, dark random buds as harsh and without sound as a suit of clams flaring. Spinning, nigger pearls, lancing aflame - rooting him at the trashcans. Such magick, that then unveiled the cocaine-white bosom of an auburn venus, switching like destiny at the periphery of disbelief.

Quinn flew to suckle her left breast, burnished with sciapods. Hot acrid milk fonting down his gullet. In the milk, sickle claws, fibrolating, weaving all through his vitals as Miss Anastasia reeled him in. He saw only the sheer chasm at night's end; felt nothing but the friction of phantoms at zero temperature. She had found the thirteenth and final member of her coven.

Back in his broken-toothed, flaming hovel, Quinn finds himself roped to the cot. Miss Anastasia is crouched above his face, her vagina mouthing sick promises in the gloom. His initiation has begun. Now, she is over his groin, licking like a cat at his circumcised erection, silken paws on his pouch. He begins to hyperventilate. Can this truly be the realisation of his wildest imaginings?

All too soon, disorder. Fungus drips from walls. The room starts to smell, like the breath of a Peeping Tom through webbed panes of meat. Whisperings and snickerings arise, darkening the horizon of his pleasure. All around him - the coven. Eleven in number, crippled, insane, wall-eyed and wasted, drooling, masturbating, braying like mules. Out comes the Nine-tails, covering Quinn with ardent kisses while Anastasia harangues the sky in a mountainous language. Her snowy eyes roll over as the assembley comes together, drenching the initiate with torpid semen. Something tears the roof off and enters, hands on hips; Quinn is vomiting like a consumptive dog. Miss Anastasia has used his libido to incur a priapic demon.

All night Quinn lies bleeding, listening to the coven revel as they watch his beloved copulate with the huge-membered demon for hours on end; listening to her unearthly cries of pleasure. Finally, her dark lover dissipates with first light; the rioters disband in silence. Alone with the Sun, Quinn resolves to raise a demon of his own.

The ability to achieve such a feat is not granted lightly. To obtain such power, Miss Anastasia ordains that he must suck at her third tit on the thirteenth day of thirteen months. She stands nude, mockingly, in front of him. Scouring her body, even probing her scalp beneath the auburn tresses, he can locate no such appendage. The watching disciples leer and snigger. Is this yet another cruel trick? Sensing his despair, Anastasia sneers, turns away from him and bends over, parting her buttocks with puce-nailed fingers. There, drooping from her occluded anus like a butcher's trinket, a coarse umber plug of flesh, dribbling brown pus, curtained by rectal hair in plaits: the supernumerary nipple. Quinn kneels and gives suck avidly, flinching at the bitter gouts of liquid faeces, the jeering of the clan. And such, for month after month, is his lot.

On the feast of the thirteenth moon, Quinn arises triumphantly from his mistress' parted haunches; his time has come. As he wipes away the sewage caking his mouth, he hops onto his bed and quickly starts to masturbate. Before the coven can react, he ejaculates the pungent seed of thirteen months' gestation, while gibbering a mangled spell. For a full minute, the room seems devoid of oxygen. Outside, a commotion of frantic mating Rottweilers; hot black light from under the floorboards. Then, from nowhere, a vast, ragged pillar of vitrified salt, and atop it a figure to terrify the assembley: Quinn has raised the very Jack of Sodom.

At once, the Jack swoops behind Miss Anastasia and roughly doubles her over; with gnarled hands he lays apart the cheeks that guard the orifice of his exaltation. A hiss of dismay flees his lips at the sight of her occult teat; then, without further ado, his jaws descend and brown teeth snip through the offending growth. Her scream recalls molten criminality, an impact of racking sin upon the immaculate. The essence of Miss Anastasia gushes forth from her uncorked breech in a deluge that bowls over the startled Jack and sluices him back into oblivion, drowned in a maelstrom of nails, pith, fins, grain, beaks, flint and pins, pods, ash, roots and stings. Only her shrunken hide survives, sloughed upon the respirating meniscus. Quinn retrieves the skin and, tugging the elastic anus over his head, wriggles up inside until it fits his rotund body like a rubber suit. He wades from the hovel regally, as if reborn.

Above, an ovation of comets. Quinn takes to the frosty backstreets in the skin of Anastasia, searching for new disciples. His progress through the broken bottles and condoms resembles a dance, an epicene ballet for shivering sects. His words are bible, his thoughts red stains. Beneath its macabre awnings, his heart flutters like a nascent vulture scenting carrion from gutter to crypt; a carnival of souls adrift on seas that crash over fiery, desolate shores - looking for love through the eyes of the Devil.

TONGUE CATHEDRAL

Sheets of vermin quit the stinking sky, the night that Meredith came home. She crossed the portico as if celebrating some profound illness, last reveller at the core of a cancerous female planet. Everything was red, saturate, turbulent. Slow. From without, noise like blurred pistons. A thirsting white rose unfurled within her elastic grid of moods, she slid from chamber to porous chamber, where men hung. Blood sliding over rubies threw opulent beads of light across her kinetic, timeless face; the memory of flighted parasites. Mercurial embers, an eccentric twist of coloured oils. Decay on jasmine breath. Kisses from a basement opiate in waves; the sensation of inexhaustible faeces gushing through an open sphincter. Repetition. A vivisectrix knows deep, orgasmic sorrows.

Her sister reclines in an ornate velvet coffin, sipping semen from baroque thimbles, slaying insects with a flick from her sickle of calcified lizards. The coffin is full of toadstools. Everywhere, sad and terrible hymns, unceasing. Bauxite. The undated bell shivers in its rat-spattered spire, announcing a traveller on horseback. In from the storm reels simple Smythe, brushing tails and pestilence from his jerkin.

Believing himself alone, he resolves to find dry clothing. A pretty dress, perhaps, or some exotic kimono embroidered with civets. Like a girl bewitched in a doll's house, he investigates each room of the mansion, trailing mauve and copper cascades of drunken light visible only to the nightcrawling eye. Body heat. The heat from a repository of sacred fluids.

Guttering, moth-bound candles imbue the halls with violet irradiance. From the arched ceiling, avian skeleta rotate blithely on chains, expelling paroxysmatic silhouettes that suggest fugue induction. Set in the tiled floor, lapis lazuli circles sprinkled with burnt offerings and soma. Each wall bears portraits of strange beings. Shadowy, transitional creatures depicted in garish acts of sado-masochism and narcissistic magick against backdrops of unchecked chaos. Envenomed images, that summon the young rider into their playground.

While the sisters dream of fluids.

Meredith licking punctured pomegranates in the gloom at the top of the stairs, peeping down at her guest like a wicked child; nothing visible save the opalescence of her teeth. Such sharp, pretty teeth, that will brook no mastication! She softly watches as her sister, whose own gums have borne no fruit, steals into the library. Feeling a fresh chill, young Smythe turns and sees her in an alcove, rippling like fire dressed in black. She gesticulates, fingering phallic avatars of tallow. Her gown is cut away about the lower belly, airing a damp triangle of hair subtly shifting by dint of infestation; a mesmeric undertow suggesting access to illimitable, concentric universes. Her red mouth, pouting and glistering with saliva, promises an eternity of hydraulic fellatio; begging for the elixir that only his loins can furnish.

The crash of a pomegranate thaws the spell; pips spurting across tomes and cheekbones recall sylphs from silver trees, sipping widow's brew in the still of a hurricane. Teasing Smythe's transvestism, Meredith proffers a choker of pulsing diamonds as she descends. Diamonds to caress that hairless male throat.

White throat filled with nectar.

Sister to sister, autumnal stares clashing across the book-lined arena, and betwixt, transfixed by slats of drilling, uncoloured light, trances in rays, their prey. Hours elapse. The foetus of new day kicking. With a giggle, Meredith relents. Her sister pounces on Smythe with a frightening embrace, peeling away his smock, her lips swallowing up his manhood. For minutes, all is still, silent but for her guzzling, his crescent whines. Finally, as his seed begins to spurt about the toothless gums, Meredith floats forward on a tide of laughter. In her slender grasp, a cobalt-handled razor, replete with bevelled blade that seems to drink in all luminosity; broiling with fathomless, assassinated urges. Hissing up from floor level, its nihilistic edge slices cleanly through poor Smythe's genitals. While her sister falls back on her haunches, bloody and oblivious, still sucking and feeding from the severed organs, Meredith basks in the virile gore that jets from the traveller's groin.

Soaked in the hot tide, blind in the final pall of night, the strands of her strange satiety conjure feline people with sad and probing tongues, mewling offspring of an eastern chant, as bells jingle from a caravan slewed across distant passes with a birthmark of campfires, raggedly outlining zones hermetic and abundant with fungal cells, mystery of milk, inside tight skin unable to comprehend the fatal law, treading pine-needles into fragrant forest lairs where fortune and history, calyx of melancholy, are tossed like heads of dark curls to a moonbeam's whim, smoke over immutable snow, unearthing coins once minted from young black fury, that now despairs beyond frost-gilded cupols of dead, and irretrievable, loss.

Sunrise.

Plumed white horses carry Meredith in her silk-lined, emerald-embossed silver casket, lid tight closed, across the yearning countryside, over the hills and far away.

THE COLOUR HELL

Daybreak hangs from East to West like a triptych of electrocuted infants, an adumbration of the church that eats its young; Katrina bowls her last grapefruit across the frozen lake. Moths erupt, tangling in her shiny, treacherous hair.

Her hair of the colour Hell.

Then back along the snow-packed bank, dragging on a rope behind her the rib-cage of the boy named Healer. On the knobbled, blanched surface of this queer sleigh she has arranged a hexagram of leveret feet, stapled to the bone. The same lucky configuration which is branded between her breasts. In seared, ridged flesh.

Flesh of the colour Hell.

It was Healer who had first introduced Katrina to Williamson. Williamson, who claimed to have been roasted alive in a motorcycle crash six winters previously; six years before rising from the grave at the behest of Healer. By night, he would tell Katrina of the sights that befell him during those years, the young girl shivering at his tales of a shade hexarchy, hung with six-edged beaten bronze talismans, that stalked the underworld; of their penchant for sowing grubs in furrows broiling with brain pulps, perpetuating the cacti whose fruit of decomposing insect protein they, and he, would devour; and of the subsequent apparitions of a fearful Jack and his servants, auto-erogenous figures compiled of wriggling limbs, organs and unclean orifices.

He told of some creatures with breasts instead of

buttocks, and double-jointed legs whose penile toes were forever lodged in the vaginas which ran down their faces like duelling-scars; some with skulls jutting on stems from their armpits to chew at lactating nipples, while their enormous phallus projected from a vulva set between trembling thigh-stumps to be encircled by a yard-long, steaming yellow tongue; some with a double torso, the first uddered with multiple penises and the second with corresponding, masturbatory hands, horses' eyeballs set in the busy fingertips; some simply inside-out, cockroaches mating on the exposed entrails while bone wombs teemed with polysexual fledgelings cut from dead skin. Spectral, ever-changing pigments in the dead biker's vision.

His vision of the colour Hell.

Soon, Katrina and Williamson were lovers. Bodies fusing under scaled epidermis as if by exchange of a million sticky oviducts, her tongue reaming volcanic sores, rectum bubbling over with ashen paste; psyches blasted by a scorching atomic wind, tidal atrophy, as they screamed the silent scream of changeling hexapods.

Healer looked on from the lonely graveyard.

Beneath the exfoliated caress of her burnt lover, Katrina came to comprehend the spectrum of the colour Hell. A spectrum diffracted from the last embers of hope as they cool on the funeral pyre, emitting from its core a host of phantom carriages that hurtle through osseous causeways, wheels ploughing liquid flesh, tearing open the arcades of the mind with a predatory, vesuvial thrust, until only the naked soul remains, pinned out on the shore of a primordial ocean that absorbs the sky, then becomes the sky, raining down untrammelled chaos; the stuff of a scope refusing to conform with gravity or the molecular, like lightning suspended in another dimension affording successive glimpses of foetuses and charnel visages, murder, stripes of metempsychosis, penetration, perfume and purulence, immolation and intelligence, defaecation, death by orgasm; eternity in a recurring microsecond.

A spectrum devoid of warmth or doubt.

A spectrum that Williamson was determined to wrest from its netherworld hexarchy and recreate above, with himself as sole high priest to the psychedelic Jack.

Healer seldom saw Katrina thereafter. Her life was spent in Williamson's hovel. One night, peering through a gap in the corrugated tin roof, Healer saw why. She was flat on her back on a filthy cot, knees splayed. From between her legs, a greasy, thrashing tentacle tipped with human thumbs, and suckered its entire length with needle-fanged mouths, was drawing its way into the world. Katrina's uterus, chirruping and plated with sentient chitin, had become a gateway for servile, transmigrant cephalopods.

More than a dozen of the creatures were already in the shack, squirming in every nook, the floorboards carpeted with inflorescent genitalia and viscera; the air visibly stagnant, almost opaque, buoyant with miraculous, unglimpsed hues. And Williamson, doyen of this mutant microcosm, leering over its fawning inmates.

Yet the Jack himself would not come forth.

Months passed. Finally, Williamson resolved to beseech the Jack in person, to bestow an offering upon him, to placate him, entice him, persuade him that far greater pleasures lay in the realms above. He would have to die again - and Healer would once more resurrect him.

On the ritual night, Healer entered the graveyard solemnly, bearing the gift of a hefty woodcutter's axe across his slender shoulders. Carefully selecting the correct headstone, he cast his spells, recalling from the dead a freshly-hanged killer. The psychopath rose before him with a head of worms; terrible breath began to filter through his macerated form. The stars went out for an instant. Then the killer snatched up the proffered axe in his wild hands, and with the aplomb of a master slaughterman he sheared off the top half of Healer's skull. While the boy's brain still sizzled in the snow, the crooning maniac gutted and jointed his sallow body. He then proceeded to reassemble it with metal cable, drag it down to the lake, and hang it from the nearest birch like a marionette. Hollowed feet scratched hoar-frost, blood blossomed on snow like a first period; on the far bank, Williamson and Katrina finished up their last supper.

Up in the branches, grinning liplessly, the psycho pulled the strings. Williamson was now peering over; he saw Healer wave, reassuringly, then plunged into the icy water, clutching the six-pronged dildo he was to present to his beloved Jack.

Williamson's bloated carcass still bobs beneath the ice, waiting for Healer to re-unite it with the soul that rots in the underworld; eaten piece by piece, violently regurgitated, then eaten up again and again in a loop of vengeance by the Jack whose pets he has stolen - just as Healer's bones are slowly consumed and recycled by the hexapods of the forest, ensuring fertility for the centuries to come.

Before Williamson's cracked, undead stare, a jubilant psychopath shoves his resurrected fist in and out of a young girl's throat, splitting open her frost-bitten lips.

Her lips of the colour Hell.

DEMON'S SPICE

In a jackal haven on the edge of town, wood-bound, traced by spits of white gravel like the uloid rivulets that fork across a vulvite starway, and mutely guarded by bone-meal sentries inset with solid gold, grinning teeth, sat Raine.

Feeding, spiny-fingered, from his cache of salted placentas; the creak of his tawny leather wings, finely brocaded with molluscs in motion, like wind around a gallows pole. Raine harboured death in every corpuscle. Yet verdant, exotic life sprang from wherever his fresh excrement fell; the rich, succulent pink stools coaxing growth even from slabs of the most unrepentant granite. Each growth, a part of his earthly garden. The garden of the white spice.

Over the centuries, Raine had established a cyclic symbiosis with the residents of the vale. He granted them the right to harvest his once forbidden flowers, which they would grind in a great wooden mill to obtain the aphrodisiac spice for use in religious orgies. And they, instantly addicted, would soon give up even their own offspring in return for more supplies. Perched atop a leafless oak, Raine would often spy on these peasants as they disported in torchlit glades, nauseated at the spectacle of their sweating, heaving bodies, the arcs of spurting juices and distended orifices, the shrieks and snarls from faces masked in still-bloody animal hides. But the results of these horrors made their licence worthwhile; the peasants' growing appetite for the spice was more than matched by a frenzied increase in copulation, and hence procreation, affording ever more infant delicacies for the demon's table. Raine disposed of the remains in secret mills of his own, providing the raw material for his coterie of smirking, gristley scarecrows. Meanwhile, his faecal sticks of the softest fat-streaked baby-meat, dropped during nocturnal prowls, fertilized ever-expanding areas of woodland with the spice-flowers.

Yet now, a veil of tears has fallen across the land. The children of generations fed on the white spice, derived as it is from the fruits of accursed lard, have developed a minimal life expectancy. Born addicts, they suckle liquid spice from the breast; so advanced is their coronary sclerosis even at such a tender age, that they invariably perish in the cot from self-induced cardiac arrest during frenzied bouts of masturbation or attempted incestuous sodomy; blue-faced babes with chest-high erections twitching in their cradle-coffins. Their meat is unpalatable, soured by tainted adrenalin. The corpsegrinder grows hungry.

Soon, the only mature townsfolk are senile, barren geriatrics; even the spice cannot induce virility, nor the flow of juices in dry hag loins. Yet still they come, scouring the woods for the scarcening blossoms, some on crutches, others raving in filthy wheelchairs. Easy prey; but not even Raine could digest their stringy, bitter-seasoned flesh.

Raine is starving. His meagre stools of greyish sludge are sterile, his fields fallen fallow. He is too weak to seek new pastures and townships. Forced to feed on his own private soldiers of ground bone and offal, he fears the onset of encephalopathy. The days spin past.

Like a spider trapped in his own web, Raine lies inert, envisioned. Looming over him, he sees a feverish parade of revellers, necrophiles and nightcrawlers with painted faces and bodies, heavily jewelled, arrayed in gaudy silks and opulent sables; bearing salvers of esoteric drugs, powdered codices, the eggs of extinct flying lizards, organisms plucked from unknown ocean citadels; exalting on a precipice pocked with craters spewing lava and boiling rock, deep within a formidable volcano, on its edge, precariously, staring down into an infernal void where all dreams cease to exist.

Winter comes.

There is an undertone to the gusting of the glacial wind; just a murmur at first, like praying basalt, or perhaps the sussuration of carnivorous petals. Growing in volume and rapidity, it soon becomes more akin to the swipe of a gigantic pendulum - a manifestation, surely, of impending death. Raine's goatish eyes focus on the shadows that flicker across his lair, trace them back to their source on the stark skyline: the four sails of the old mill, untethered, stirred into action for the first time in decades.

No doubt it was just the wind that blew them free, snapping the rotted ropes.

No doubt.

But then again, there is one other possibility. Perhaps the sails were freed by hand. Human hand. What if a secret herd of these prey-animals still flourishes beneath the ruined township, glutted on covert arks of the holy anther?

Drawing on his very last pools of dwindling energy, Raine lopes, half air-borne, across fields of clean-picked skeletons clutching pastel fossilized flowers, to the mill.

In its lichen-spotted basement, atop a drift of freshly-ground spice, Raine espies two figures. They are evidently children, a boy and girl, emaciated, vagabond waifs no more than ten years old; escapees, judging by the hideous burns along their naked bodies, from the ovens of some cannibal overlord in a nearby valley. Possessed by the spice, they remain unaware of Raine as he peers down from the rafters.

The boy is lying flat on his back, while the girl squats over him, her haunches in his face, sucking at the head of his over-enlarged penis; he pulling her buttocks apart with his fingertips, thrusting his tongue deep into her rifled rectum. As ever, Raine is sickened by the sight, sound and stench of his cattle in sexual delirium. He sees the sears on the girl's back open up, lined with carious incisors; the boy's mane is bolt upright, knotted in electric runes. The pair seem halo'ed by blazing giblets.

Raine swoops. Weak, he lands awkwardly, kicking over a brazier of burning pitch. The carpet of seed-husks ignites at once, engulfing all.

For a day and a night they watched the old mill burn from neighbouring hillsides. Then the black, intoxicating smoke settled in the vales like fog, filling the lungs, precipitating a wild and month-long debauch.

A thick, oily soot, all that remained of the demon and his spice, seeped into soil and stone alike; into the gills of fish in fast-flowing estuaries, into the fodder and bellies of beasts, and thence into the craw of migrant, coprophagic birds; into the wind, and the thunder, and into the very fibre of the planet.

ZODIAC BREATH

In the time it takes for one man to masturbate in his lonely bed, a million stars burn out; a million more are born.

Rivers wend their way to sea, blades trace the curve of backbones under white and virgin skin.

Tonight, we have no sense of crime.

Appendix

RAISM

The Songs of Gilles de Rais

Meathook Seed

PLEASURES PAVE SEWERS.
WHO BELONG DEAD, FOLLOW.

EVERY DITCH IS A NIGHT SCAR, PLATED WITH BABY BONES,
THE INFECTED SPOKES OF A STAR REPOSITORY.
A SULPHUROUS PLANET VENTS BLESSINGS; THE DEAD KNOW
DREAMS.
FROM A MEATHOOK I SING OF LIFE ORBITED BY DARK METEORS,
SACRIFICED TO THE EXTERMINATION OF THE HUMAN FAMILY.
SONGS FROM A HOWLING HEAD, INFESTED WITH REPTILE DOLLS.
MY MIRROR HAS FATHOMLESS, ECSTATIC QUADRANTS.
IN THE FIRST, AN ODE TO THE SUCTION OF YOUNG MAIDENS
CONCEALING A CONQUERING WORM WITHIN ITS ROSE.
THE SECOND RELAYS BEHESTS FROM KINGS FURLED IN VASES,
SUNKEN PSALMS, LICKING UP THE FAECES OF THE DEVIL
DRIVING DAGGERS THROUGH MY MIND.
THROUGH THE THIRD, PUCKERED PROJECTIONS IMBUED WITH
THE ANGULAR FEAR OF COPULATING CHILDREN SEEK SHELTER
FROM THE SWIPE OF THE PENDULUM.
IN THE FOURTH, ARCADES WHERE THE SOUL IS ORDAINED TO A
SECT OF SHIVERS, HOURS SEDUCED IN ENAMEL CASKS,
PUNISHING IN DESOLATE LOOPS THE STAINING OF THE WHITE
SPADIX.

THUNDER LIGHTS THE CAVELANDS WHERE MY FAMILIAR CALLS
FROM A COTTON CRUISE.
WISE SPITS IMPART A GLOTTAL CABBALA, DEPICTING
A WANDERER OVERHUNG BY DEAD BEASTS ON CORDS;
SEEKING VINDICATION IN AROUSAL, RAPTURES, THE TORQUE OF
NUBILE HIPS, EQUINE NATIVITY, THE COITION OF SWANS.
I DRAW DIVINATIONS FROM THE PHRENOLOGY OF CANTHARIDS;

THROUGH A SAFFRON HAZE I SEE ALL MOTHERS AND TRAITORS INCINERATED ON INFERNAL SKEWERS.
DAWN DISROBES IN ELEGAIC COILS, A SKYLINE OF VAINGLORIOUS BLUES, DEMONOGRAPHIC, CORRUGATED WITH WWHEELS ERECTED FOR TRUCIDATIONS OF THE JUDGED.
IN THE CHATEAU OF THE WORM: A LUCIFUGE PITTED AGAINST THE GRAIN, ATTENUATED BY A CONCATENATION OF SINS BURNT ONTO SILKEN TREATIES, PACTS BETWEEN CRETIN ARCHANGELS AND REAPERS.
THE CONJUGAL CHAMBERS ARE CLUTTERED WITH PELAGIC BOUNTY, COFFIN INNARDS, EWERS OF BABY FINGERS AND DRIED DOG ROSES, A PROSTITUTE MOTIF IN PULMONARY HUES.
NAILED TO A CROSS FOR THE CRIME OF CONCEPTION, THE NUDE SHAVEN BRIDE FECUNDATED ON A WOLF RUN.
HER ENORMOUS BELLY IS A TRANSFIGURED CONTINENT, CENTURIES OF INCEST MAGNIFIED.
ARTERIES BURST APART AS SCORBUTIC PAWS EXTRUDE BELOW, THICK WITH ECTOPIC PARASITES, TEARING OPEN GUTTERING NATAL MEAT AND THIGH FAT UNDER A RAIN OF BLOOD CLOTS TEXTURED LIKE HERPETIC MELONS.
SCREAMS CONGEAL IN DRIPPING RECEPTACLES.
A SIAMESE QUADRUPED SPRAWLS FORTH ON A HAIR HOSE, CONJOINED AT SNOUT AND SCROTUM.
FURIOUS AT THIS CLANDESTINE INTERUTERINE SYMPHYSIS, THE PROGENITOR DASHES TWIN DEFORMED SKULLS ONTO STONE AND THEN SETS TO WITH POIGNARDS; HANGING THE HACKED FRAMES HIGH ON A NET OF FUSED BLUBBERS.
KILLING IS A SEXUAL CLOAK, DRAWN ABOUT THE SHOULDERS THE WAY RAVENS PRAY IN VESUVIAL NIGHT.
TRUE FAITH IS THE SLAUGHTER OF INFANTS WHO WOULD ELSE GROW INTO PRIESTS, GAOLERS, HUSBANDS OR MOTHERS, LIARS, CENSORS, EXCREMENT-HATERS.
HOOKS FLY FROM DEAD SATELLITES TO BRAKE THE ASCENDENCY OF THE MORNING SUN; A MILLION SHADES VAULT THROUGH THE DISORDERED SOLAR SYSTEM.
HENCEFORTH, ALL LIFE IS CALIBRATED BY THE RISE AND FALL OF HATCHETS.

I, GILLES de RAIS, DITCHFINDER GENERAL, PINK VENUS RAG-BURNER, HEADSMAN HARVESTING CANNIBAL TAR-BABIES WHOSE VENEREAL TOPIARY LATTICES THE FUR PORTALS OF HARRIDANS BENT ON AUTO-SODOMISATION WITH SHRIEKING WAX EFFIGIES OF ABORTED PROGENY;

FREAK MAGGOT DONKEY THRASHER TENDING SPHINCTERS THAT
BLAST FORTH THE ANTHROPOMORPHIC CHILDREN OF OUR BASEST
DESIRES, FACE BUTCHER WHOSE STELLAR APIARIES DISCHARGE
HORNETS INTO SILVER NIGHTMARE SPERM CAVERNS;
TWILIGHT ARSONIST SUCKING SEED FROM CROPPED BLACK SOWS
ON THE CUSP OF WHIPCORD, TRENCH-SHARPENED SKULLCRAWLER
EATING RODENT SKELETA IN THE TOWER OF ENEMAS;
INFANT OFFAL MAGUS FIRING THE THROBBING BONES OF A
NARCOTIC ORGASM SLAUGHTER, CHARNEL-FINGERS, KING OF THE
JACKAL HOLE JERKING HIGH ON A NOOSE OF OSSIFIED SEMEN.

ICICLES OF BLOOD ON YOUR BARRED HOVEL WINDOWS,
NORTH OF A MOON AT ITS ZENITH OF LUPINE DELINQUENCY;
PARRICIDAL JAWS DRAGGING TRUTH DISMEMBERED TO YOUR
TABLE; FEAST ON MY PUMPING FLESH, ITS LIBIDINOUS
ELIXIRS, IF YOU CRAVE COMPANY WITH VIRULENT LIFE OVER
ITS ARID SEMBLANCE.
YOUR VIRGIN EARS CANNOT ESCAPE DEPUCELATION BY MY
SLAVERING TESTIMONIAL; THE MAIMING EVANGELISM OF
de RAIS AMID THE RUINS.
SKIN BIBLE CODICES INDICATE CYCLIC METEMPSYCHOSIS.
BEHOLD A LIFE DEDICATED TO WOLF SEX IDOLATRY, DOGGING
THE SCARLET FETISH FOR TRANSCENDENTAL GLIMPSES.
TRUE EXISTENCE IS ENDLESS METAMORPHOSIS AND ORGASM,
A CIRCLE OF PAROXYSMS CHARGED WITH MUTANT BEAUTY.
INSATIABLE PROMISCUITY OF THE SOUL DRIVES THE DITCH
VISIONARY TO DEFINE AN ELLIPTIC PORNOGRAPHY, GIVING
REIN TO THE CALIGULATE CHROMOSOME; WATCHFIRES SET IN
DORSAL DOMAIN GUIDING HOMICIDAL INSTINCTS HOME,
PERFORATING THE MAGNOLIA CURTAIN.
THE KILLER SPRINGS FROM THE FROZEN STEPPES, A TOUCH-
STONE OF OPIUM AND SILVER DEEP IN HIS FUNDAMENT;
TRAILING A SPOOR OF DUNG, BONES AND SEMEN, AN INDELIBLE
PHOSPHORESCENCE OUTSHINING EVEN THE BOREAL LIGHTS ON A
WINTER'S SOLSTICE.
EMBRACE THE DITCHFINDER, SWALLOW HIM WHOLE, THAT A TWO-
HEADED SOW MIGHT BURST FROM YOUR HEART AT COCK-CROW.
COME FORTH THEN AND GROVEL BENEATH, CATCHING IN YOUR
CRAW MY RANK RABIES SPITTLE, SUCKLING THE JUICY PIZZLE
WHOSE SORES WEEP THE STUFF OF FAITHS UNKNOWN TO YOUR
KIND.
HERE, BURIED TO THE HILT IN FILTH, YOU MAY GLIMPSE THE
IMMUTABLE HORROR THAT MY SWEET HOWLS CONVEY; YOU MAY

DETECT THE DEATH RATTLE DRAWING ALL TO THIS TERMINUS.
I SING OF THE SUFFOCATING DENSITY OF MATTER, SOULS AS
REFLECTORS DISTORTING THE NEGATIVE VELOCITY OF MORTAL
MASS; WHITE MEAT FEVER, THE UNENDURABLE TORMENT OF
DRAWING BREATH THAT DELUDED MANKIND DEEMS DIVINE.
THE CURSE OF THE RAVEN, THE MARK OF THE BEAST - MAN
AND WOMAN ALIKE ARE BRANDED WITH STIGMATA OF
INTOLERABLE DEGRADATION.
DOWN HERE, SOAKED IN MY COLD PREACHER SPEW, YOU WILL BE
PRIVY TO VERTIGINOUS INSURRECTIONS AGAINST NATURE.
TO YIELD NOW INCURS DAMNATION, A SWELTERING ETERNITY
INSIDE YOUR FEEBLE, LEADEN CARCASS.
MY FURNACE CORPSE BREATH, AS TORRID AS THE EJACULATION
OF A GARROTTED LUNATIC, URGES YOU INSTEAD TO SEEK
COMMUNION WITH THE GROUND, TO BANQUET ON THE WEALTH OF
INNER OCEANS, REVELLING IN THE ASTRAL CUNNILINGUS OF
THE LYCANTHROPE.

IN MONUMENTAL EVENING, A CYCLONE OF DILDOS TEMPERED
FROM A TAURUS VANE; DOOMED CHATELAINE.
THE DITCHFINDER SKINS THE SKULL OF HIS SEVENTH WIFE,
THREADS COPPER WIRE THROUGH THE DEATHMASK AND SECURES
THE RITUAL DEVICE AROUND HIS HIPS, FORMING A MOIST WARM
POUCH FOR HIS GENITALS.
BY THE LIGHT OF CORUSCATING OVENS HE SAWS THROUGH THE
CRANIUM, EXPOSING THE CONVULSIVE BRAIN, THEN DEFAECATES
OVER THE SLICK EPIDURIS.
EXCREMENT AND CEREBRAL AMOEBAE DISSOLVE AND MERGE,
COAGULATING INTO NECROMANTIC DIAGRAMS, THE IMPRESSION
OF A MINK FUTURE.
ON AN OAKEN DAIS, A MENSTRUATING ADOLESCENT GIRL IS
ARCHED ON ALL FOURS LIKE A CRAB, NIPPLES RAKING SKY-
WARD.
PRONE AMID VOTIVE NARCISSI, I HEAR THE METABOLIC MOON
IN SOLILOQUY, FEEL ITS SARDONIC ETIOLATION AND SLY
CALCIUM ADDICTIONS UNTIL MY PELVIS CASTS A LUPINE
SHADE.
I POUNCE, SNIFFING THE GIRL'S TURBID WATERS, MY TWO
FRONT PAWS DABBLING IN THE RIVULETS ON HER WIDE OPEN
THIGHS; MY TENDER MUZZLE INVADES DISTENDED SCARLET
LIPS, FURROWING SEAMS THAT YIELD INGOTS OF FLAYED LOTUS
INCARNATE.
EYES, ONCE CRUSTED WITH PARCHED LOATHING, NOW

LACRIMATE, DILATING UNDER TUMULTS OF COSMIC SAPPHIRE
AS I MOUNT HER.
MY SNOUT CLAMPS ABOUT HER FACE, TUBULAR INCISORS
CUTTING DEEP TO SUCK SWEET FAT FROM HER CHEEKS, MOLARS
CRUNCHING NASAL CARTILAGE; I SHOOT A TETANUS SEED DEEP
INSIDE, THEN MANGLE THE GURGLING REMAINS.

COLOURED RAINS BOIL THROUGH A BESTIAL HOOP, MY
ELONGATED THORAX RINGING WITH CACOPHONIC HYPODERMAL
PERCUSSION, SENSES SHOT BENEATH A RED RHAPSODY;
A RICTUS OF GLIMPSES WHERE TRIPLE SIX SUCK ANGELS
FLICKER WINGS OF VELVET ANNIHILATION OVER LAKES THE
SHAPE OF LUST, FLAMING TULPAS LAUNCHED FROM CAT PUPA
FONTANELLES, GHOSTS OF AN UNDERBELLY FIREWORK GROOVE;
A CRADLE INVOCATION OF MAGENTA PHOBIAS, NOMAD SPIRAL
INTO SLOW-BLEED GORGON LATITUDES, TARANTELLA OF OPAL
SCARABS ON A VIJ VERTIGO HELIX; ALL CREEP AND CRAWL
IN THE SHADOW OF THE VALLEY OF GRISTLE.
PULPED BY INTERNAL COMPRESSION;
VERTEBRAE FLY FROM A CRUMPLED BACKBONE, BLIZZARD OF
TEETH FROM SICK RECEDING GUMS. CLUMPS OF SILVER FUR
MATERIALISE THROUGH NAKED MUSCLE, FOLLICLES ROOTED IN
MARROW.
TORRENTIAL PAIN, A CARMINE LITANY IN REVERSE, AS THE
REBEL TEGUMENT PEELS ITSELF FROM MY BODY AND LOPES INTO
THE FAR SYLVAN BEYOND GENERATING MALFORMED APPENDAGES;
THE AUTOMIMESIS OF A VARGAMOR DYNASTY PRIMED FOR
PAGANISM.

THE TANNED HIDE OF BUTCHERED BRIDES MAKES THE MOST
PERFECT VESTMENT - BUT THOSE WITH SOFT LEATHER SKIN
AND FUR ENTRAILS HAVE LITTLE NEED OF CLOTHING.
MY TRUE FAMILY IS RISEN - THE PACK, OUR TRAGIC
CANTICLES COMMEMORATING HEADY PREHISTORIC MOONS, BLOOD
RIVERS, SISTERS SODOMISED IN THE SNOW.
FED WITH PHILTRES FROM THE SEEDED RUT, OUR RELENTLESS
DEPREDATIONS DECIMATE THE VILLAGES AND VAGRANT HERDS OF
SICKLY CHRISTIAN CATTLE, DRIVING THE SORRY DREGS TO
REFUGE IN SACKCLOTH AND LEPROSY.
THEIR WOMENFOLK ARE RAVISHED AND EATEN BY RENEGADE
WOLVERINES WITH LAUGHING HUMAN HEADS FOR TESTICLES;
VULPINE VAMPIRES, RAMPANT SEWER FOXES WITH FOUR
SWIVELLING JAWS OF HOLLOW IVORY NEEDLES, DRINK UP THE

BRAINS OF SLEEPING YOUTHS.
FERAL MADNESS STALKS THE FOREST IN A HEX OF HEARTS, ATTENDED BY MEAT-CREATURES CAGED IN TRANSLUCENT EXO-SKELETONS; ROVING FROM HILL TO HAMLET, SCALING EVERY BLIND CORNICE TO TRAP AND DESTROY ECCLESIASTIC QUARRY.
MY IMPERIAL WARP CONFINES THE RIGHTEOUS TO THEIR MILLS AND SILENT BELFRIES, A VOLATILE VENOM AGENT, PELLUCID GENESIS OF TUMOUR.
SPINES ASSAILED BY A RABID ALIEN, GELDED MINISTERS COMB SCRIPTURES FOR SALVATION.
DESPERATION GARNERS GAUNT REWARD.
GENOCIDE, SEAS OF FLAME, SKIES BLACKENED BY PLAGUE-BEARING VERMIN; THE EARTH SPLIT BY CREVICES GLUTTED WITH HYMENOPTERAN SHE-DEVILS, HERALDS OF A BEHEMOTH CARAPACED IN FLAWED AMETHYST WHOSE POSTERIOR OVIDUCTS SECRETE THE GERM OF A THOUSAND COWLED MORROWS.

TODAY OUR INCURSIONS INFLAME A PAUPER SETTLEMENT ALREADY VISITED BY THE CROPPED BLACK SOW.
MY HARRIER HOGS ROOT INSURGENTS FROM MEADOWS; SOLDIERS NAIL MENFOLK UPTURNED ON CROSSES, PUT FIRE TO THEIR FACES.
COMMUNING WITH HORSE, I UNCOVER A COVEN OF PREGNANT WIVES HUDDLED IN MANGERS.
ONE, PASSING BOTTLED NIGHTMARES IN AND OUT OF HER BREASTS, RELATES TO ME IN HER TERROR THE TALE OF HOW THE DEVIL CAME TO HER ONE NIGHT AND COVERED HER, WHILE HIS SEPTIC SLUT PACK PEELED THE SKIN AND MEAT FROM HER HUSBAND'S DORMANT BONES TO FEED THEIR HELLHOUNDS.
UNSPEAKABLY AROUSED BY THIS EVOCATION OF WANTON PENETRATION, I FALL UPON THE WOMAN.
CARVING OPEN HER GROTESQUE STOMACH, I EXTRICATE THE STINKING FOETUS THAT LURKS WITHIN, A VIVIFIED, SIMPERING CINDER.
OILED WITH AQUEOUS ANTENATAL BITUMEN, I PERPETRATE VIOLATIONS UPON THE ASHLING THAT AFFORD A SENSATION OF STATIC SPACE TRAVEL, TANGIBLE NEGATIVES, THE FRICTION OF PHANTOMS AT ZERO TEMPERATURE.
YOKES OF ENTITY BUCKLE LIKE IRON BUTTER, BECKONING UNNATURE.

BLACK MOON, DEVIL'S GOLD.
I, AN INQUISITOR EXISTING SOLELY TO SPLIT COLD LIPS.

VIANDS TURN TO PLATTERS OF PULING EXCRETA BEFORE MY
GAZE; CARNATIONS COMBUST, CASTING THE STILLBORN DIE.
CANINE MYSTICS COVET CODES DERIVED FROM ANTELOPE BONES
IN MOONSTRUCK POOLS, THROUGH WHOSE MENISCUS MY FACE IS
AN ABSCESS SET WITH TEN OSCULATING ANUS-EYES, POITRINE
A CONTAGION CACHE STOWED BY THE AGARIC MUSE.
WITH STUMPS I STROKE A BASKET-BEARING MADONNA RAPED IN
THE CRADLE, FASCINATED BY THE PROTOZOIC BARBARISM
WITHIN THE DOWN OF HER COOL, MURDEROUS NAPE.
HER SOAKING SEX OFFERS LIFE IN A BELL-JAR, A LABIAL
SIRROCO EVOKING EULOGIES TO HOLY PROSTITUTION; IN THE
FLOES OF A MUCAL MERIDIAN, SPRINKLING GRAVES WITH
QUARTERED CHERUBS.
TUNED TO TREMORS, THE TRIANGULAR STORM DOUBLES.
ALL THE DEVILS ARE REBORN, DANCING WITH THE ELEGANCE OF
BURNING CHILDREN.
THE BLOODTHIRSTY TREE IS HUNG WITH FORSAKEN HUNTERS,
HALOED IN HIVES LIKE PRIMORDIAL MEDALS SPELLING
SEDITION.
ALL LOVERS SUFFUSED WITH CANCERS BY A PETULANT OLIVE
BRUISE; SIRIUS DESCENDANT.
TAWNY PADS GENTLY LOWER MY EYELIDS; OUR EXTERMINATION
BECOMES THE GLUTTONOUS COPULATION OF SKULLCRAWLERS.
HATE, AN ELEMENTAL BANE, GUSTS ACROSS THE HALLUCINANT
TERRAIN; MOUNTAINS MEET THEIR MAKER.
BEHOLD A LAND WHERE SEXLESS MISERY TRAMPS CLUTCH AT
BUTTOCKS BEYOND THEIR COMPREHENSION, WHERE WOMEN SHUN
CHILDHOOD SUITORS TO FORNICATE WITH DEMONOLATORS IN
DISUSED KENNELS.
A BRAYING CUPID THANATOS LOOSED FROM ARCTURIAN STABLES
THUNDERS THIS WAY, HELLBOUND AND RIDDEN BY GHOSTS IN
FLAMES.
THE SHAMBLING STARS CRY VENGEANCE.
THE FUTURE IS A ROTTED ASS TETHERED TO NEMESIS, CROSSED
BY THE MARK OF THE SUN THIEF.
FROM THE BATTLEMENTS I SEE TALL TREES BOW TO THE
BESERKER, A PERMANENT INTERNECINE WINTER, DEVASTATION.
A MILLION KILLING SEEDS JET THROUGH THE COLLECTIVE
OESOPHAGUS; ALL CURSES TRIPLE.

THE CRIES OF BEASTS ARE INFINITELY MORE ELOQUENT THAN
THE ABSURD VERBIAGE OF MAN, A RETARD FOREVER
QUESTIONING THE INSTANT.

COUNTLESS LIPS AND TONGUES OF QUERULOUS PEASANTS HANG ON STRINGS FROM MY NURSERY CEILING; JUXTAPOSED WITH THE WATTLES OF FOWL, THESE EXCISIONS COMPOSE A KINETIC CAUL FOR MY CAVE OF TOYS.
STOOPED OVER A CRACKLING LODESTONE, MY REFULGENT BREECH LAUNCHES A BATTERY OF ANTHROPOMORPHIC STOOLS ALOFT. SOME ARE INTERCEPTED BY THE PRESCIENT JAWS OF WHIPPETS; THE SURVIVORS ALIGHT NIMBLY ON THE SLATE FLOOR AND BEGIN TO JIG AND PRANCE AROUND THE HEARTH, HUMMING BITTER RHYMES.
JUMPING JACKS UNFURL FROM BOXES OF CATARRH, MARIONETTES MICTURATE OVER CRUCIFIED SQUIRRELS.
CHILL LIGHT SCINTILLATES FROM A SILL OF SUGARCANE SKULLS.
BAD SCARECROWS POUND AT THE CHAMBER DOOR, STUNG BY THE HOAR WITHOUT; ROOKS PECK OUT FOX-EYES IN THE FALLOW. LUPERCALIA COMES ORCHESTRATED BY HAVOC AND HER COHORTS, TAILDRAGGERS TILTING AT OBLIVION, THRESHOLD RAMBLERS WHO HAVE ABANDONED THEIR DEMON AND FALLEN FROM GRACE WITH ATROCITY.
DRINK FROM THE BUTT OF GLAUCOMA, SWILLING GOURDS OF FATAL DIAMETER; THE SAPPHIC PSYCHOSECRETIONS OF MY SISTER MOONS IN CONJUNCTION WILL DESCRIBE A METEOROLOGIC CRESCENT RAINING PITILESSLY THROUGHOUT YOUR PSYCHIC GUTTERS.
THE SIREN IS WHIPPED AND RACKED, DOGS LAPPING SWEAT FROM HER RELIGIOUS NAVEL; THE MAIDENHEAD OF MIDNIGHT HANGS IN TATTERS.
DITCH LOCATORS RIDE LAWLESSNESS, HARNESSING VICTIMS WITH PRAYERS WHISPERED IN A TRENCH PARLANCE KNOWN ONLY TO THE SHADOW, PHANTASMS OF A CIRCUMCISED BRAIN HOLDING RIOTS IN THE FACE.
VELVET HOLES APPEAR AND CLOSE.
AN ENORMOUS BLACK SHARK IS RISEN FROM THE MIGHTY OCEAN, SIGHTLESS, VERSED IN MYSTERIES YOU WILL NEVER GLIMPSE. JUST AS A JUVENILE TYRANT DRAWS HOOKS THROUGH HIS MOTHER'S BREAST AND WINCHES HER TO THE RAFTERS WHILST PROCLAIMING THAT BEYOND A GATE OF PENSIVE BEETLE FORCEPS LIES NADIR, SO GILLES de RAIS DENOUNCES WOMAN-KIND FROM HIS BLUE DELTA; ROASTING THE SHE-RAT ON EVERY SYLLABLE, BLACK MASS VELOCITY SCORPION IN THE LEATHER FANGS OF MISOGYNY.
IT IS THE EVE OF DEAD SOULS.

Moon Scar

WALPURGISNACHT.
A BIFURCATE TAIL STRIKING SPARKS FROM THE FLINT COURTYARD AFFORDS A FLASH OF SHRIVELLED BLACK MEAT WITH YELLOW EYES, THE HEPATIC TONGUE TAKING NOURISHMENT FROM THE BROTH OF OUR BOWELS; CRUEL BREATH DAUBING MY CEREBRAL CANVAS WITH THE PORTRAIT OF A RANCID MAIN BEYOND THIS PRISON OF AGEOMETRIC OBSIDIAN.
A GIGANTIC SHARK, BUOYED ON THE FOAMING EBB TIDE, VOMITS FORTH A LIMBLESS NAVIGATOR WHO PROCLAIMS THAT THE WORLD IS BUT AN EGG OF DUNG ENWREATHED BY DANK WORMS. HIS CONTORTED MOUTH RECALLS THE LIVIDITY OF NUNS RAVISHED BY THE PHALLIFORM CRUCIFIX.
CHAINED, CALLIPYGOUS SIRENS PERFORM, ACCOMPANIED BY THE SPLAYED GALLOP OF AMPHIBIOUS COLTS NECKLACED IN TEETH OF THE SEA.
DISCORPORATED ON THE BEACH, WE WITNESS THE CONCENTRIC VIOLENCE OF OUR HEARTH AND HOUSEHOLD GODS.

ON THIS ENTROPIC NIGHT MY FAUCAL DELIGHTS THREATEN TO RAVAGE THE VERY FIRMAMENT AND ITS ANNIHILATING STARS; THE CRAZED RETORT OF MY SISTERS COWERS THE WICKED ICE FORESTS.
OUR SONG ASCENDS HEAVENWARD ON A GLACIAL SPUME, CONFIGURATION DEATH AS A PITCH MOON REELS OVER THE HORIZON, CRIMSON-VEINED LIKE A CHEESE OF PUTRID MEAT.
DOWN IN THE WOODS THE NECROPHILE FROLICS WITH HIS RIGID CONSORTS, AUBURN PELT ABRIM WITH LEECHES, DRY ULCERATED TONGUE THIRSTING FOR THE MILK OF RECTAL PARTURITION.
FACELESS TAR-BABIES SUCKLE THE THIRD TIT OF THEIR WITCH DAM, PLUG OF COARSE TISSUE ON HER PLUCKED PUBIS SURMOUNTING THE SULPHUR LIPS OF A ROTTEN MEAT CHASM STITCHED TIGHT WITH COPPER THREAD.

MAGICK CHARMS, CHICKEN-BONES AND EFFIGIES DANGLE FROM THE TWISTED SUTURES.
IMAGINE THE WILDEST REVELATIONS OF A NIGHTCRAWLER BLASTED BY FORKED LIGHTNING AS HE DEFAECATES OVER A FRESHLY-SKINNED SKULL: SUCH ARE AS NOUGHT WHEN COMPARED TO THESE NOCTURNAL TABLEAUX.
WHERE BILE FROM WITCHCRAFT LIPS SPLASHES THE GROUND, THE SCORCHED EARTH CRASHES ASUNDER TO SPIT BACK THE BONES OF SODOMISED INFANTS.
WE BREATHE IN, BREATHE OUT, BREATHE IN THE FOETID AURA OF GRAVEYARD EROTICA.
THE DITCHFINDER LICKS THE TOUCHSTONE NEWLY-PRISED FROM HIS CAECUM, PEARL OF A CENTURY-LONG GESTATION.
THE PRODUCT OF SODOM, THIS RARE NUGGET LENDS ITSELF TO DELECTABLE ALCHEMY.
LIKE A FATHER HOARDING STRANGE EGGS FROM THE FILIAL CUCKING- BOWL, SHIVERING IN RAYS OF WAN ROMANCE, THE COPROMAGE TRANSMUTES BASE MATTER FROM HIS UNRAVELLED VISCERA INTO GLISTERING ARMOUR FIT FOR LUNAR DEITIES.
ALL SUBSTANCE IS PROFOUNDLY ILLUMINATED; THE VALUE OF DUNG BECOMES EVIDENT EVEN TO THE EYE OF A PRIEST.

GREETINGS FROM THE TORTURE GARDENS AT TIFFAUGES, WHERE PRELATES AND NUNS ARE CLAMPED IN PILLORIES OF SCAR TISSUE.
SOULS LOCKED IN A DISEASED CONUNDRUM, OUR PROGRESS IS THAT OF PIRATE SEEDS THROUGH OCEANIC SLIME CURTAINS, TOILING UNDER A PRECIPITATION OF AUTO-EROTIC ECTOPLASM, SPECTRAL SCAVENGERS IN SUPPURATING LEATHER.
GLOBES OF ANCIENT SEMEN SCATTER LIKE MARBLES ACROSS THE FLAGSTONES OF MY FACE; I KISS THE VISCOUS EYES OF A DOG FURRED IN FLIES, PESTILENTIAL HARBINGER OF THE DEVIL HIMSELF ON HIS PALANQUIN OF RATS AND LIVING SICKNESS.
MY FACE IS A COMBUSTION OF OYSTER FAT AND UNTAMED LEPER MEAT. ONE HUNDRED FRIGID WINTERS HAVE I SAILED THIS MAIN OF ORDURE, RIDDLED WITH BELLYWORMS AND COPROPHAGIC LICE. SMEARED IN CAMPHOR, APRICOT PULPS AND ABSINTHE, FINGERTIPS WAXED WITH UNGUENTS PARED FROM THE MANDIBLES OF WASPS ASPHIXIATED OVER CHARRED DIAMONDS, I TOY WITH DIAPHANOUS PEARLS TORN FROM THE SCROTAL CLAMS OF CORSAIRS BUT ONE HOUR DEAD ON THE YARDARM.
MOUNTED ON DECAYING MULES THE COLOUR OF DESIRE, A PACK OF TIMBERWOLVES RUN GAUNTLETS BENEATH MY SKIN, MY

MUSCLES RIPPLING WITH VEGETABLE ANAMORPHOSIS;
MY SAD METAL BONES CLIMB HELIUM CHAINS LOWERED FROM THE
HONEY-COATED CRAGS OF SATURN.
CADAVERS LEAP FROM URINE VATS AT THE CLATTER OF FALLEN
STAR- MANTLES, SOULS OUT OF FOCUS URGING A GUT
METALLURGY, GOLD SEEPS FROM DEMON SPHINCTERS.
JACKALS IN HUMAN MASKS BURST STEAMING AND IRIDIUM-
TOOTHED FROM THE BELLY OF A STALLION, SPINNING ON HIND
LEGS, DROOLING SHRILL MAGGOTS ON A TRIP INTO THE
LABYRINTHINE TESTES OF THE WORM.
THE BLACK MEAT IS ABROAD.
THE HOWLING OF FLOWERS THAT HANG IN DESOLATE CRYPTS
PREFIGURES AN APPARITION OF MAD THORNS, IMPALING THE
MOON ON ITS CRUEL RAMPART; THE RUPTURED RIND DISCHARGES
DEW WHICH EXPLODES LIKE LIQUID COPPER ARTILLERY,
COATING BOUGHS WITH ILLICIT BLOSSOM AND SHOWERING DOWN
AN IRRADIANT LADDER TO FORBIDDEN DOMES WHERE VAMPIRES
LANGUISH AMID INCONTINENT ARCHITECTURE, ULTRAVIOLET
FLESH STAGNATING UNDER SHEER, DELIQUESCENT DERM.
BRIDES CROWNED IN NIGHTSHADE TIARAS SWING FROM
ARABESQUE TOPAZ GIBBETS, WATCHED BY UNDEAD SENTINELS IN
GAUZE MAZES; FURNITURE OF SHANKBONES STEEPED IN BITTER
ALOES, GARLANDED WITH CORONETS OF SPURGE AND PURSLANE,
AWASH WITH TINCTURES OF STORAX, NITRE AND ARSENIC.
A TEMPLE OF MORTAL EMBERS, INTERSPERSED WITH FIGURINES
OF PHORA AND RHIZOPHAGUS.
LONG-DEAD TREES CREAK AND SWAY, ENGORGED WITH DIABOLIC
ADRENALIN, AS NECROMANCERS WEAVE AN INVOCATION OF
INSANITY FROM VICIOUS, UNCHARTED ZODIACS.
AN AMORPHOUS BEAST OF SLAVERING OFFAL DWELLS IN THE EYE
OF THE STORM, HEWING ITS WED POD FROM SICK MEMBRANE,
SEETHING WITH THE HISS OF URIC ACID ON BARE INCUBUS
BONE. FATHOMLESS PUPILS COALESCE LIKE BLACK MERCURY IN
EYES THAT ARE PHANTASMAGORIC SMEARS REFLECTING A
MILLENNIUM OF ANIMAL REGENERATION THROUGH BLOODY
GLACIERS, RUBY PRISMS WASHING LIGHT OVER FERAL SECLUDED
FACES; SUCCUBI THAT CLING TO CHAMBER WALLS WITH CLAWS
BROKEN AND RIMED IN RECTAL MUCUS, LABIA CLOTTED WITH
PRIAPIC RESINS, PUBIC PLAITS SNAGGLED WITH GORE-GLAZED
PIG-TEETH.
ALL HELL IS ABROAD, LOOSED FROM FOREST LAIRS CARPETED
IN WOLFBANE AND MANDRAGORA; CROOKED CROSSES AND PURPLE
AFTERBIRTHS DRAPED OVER SODDEN, DEFILED GRAVES.

THE DEADLY VISITATION ACCENTUATES FELINE VESTIGES; PURRING SIX-NIPPLED GIRLS SHRED THE TENSED BACKS OF THEIR FATHERS.
POSSESSED CHILDREN DRINK EACH OTHER IN CYCLAMEN AND HIBISCUS GLADES, UNDEAD SISTERS DESICCATE BROTHERS BY THE TOLL OF THE HUNCHBACK BELL.
BLASPHEMOUS MAN-CUBS BURROW INTO HUMUS WOMBS, WEANED ON A MILK OF MOONS, UNTIL THE HURRICANE SIGNALS VERNAL REVENGE.

CHILDREN ARE THE LOWEST FORM OF CREATION, MUD EFFIGIES EXCRETED FROM STINKING HINDQUARTERS BY THOSE TOO BASE OR VEGETATIVE TO PRODUCE THE TRUE, CEREBRAL OFFSPRING OF ART OR SCIENCE.
THESE WRETCHED PARENTS THEN ABUSE AND ASSAULT THE RESULT OF THEIR SQUALID COLLUSION - ASSASSINATING LIBERTY.
THE DITCHFINDER BIDS RISE TO A NEW RACE, NURTURED ON THE DEBAUCHED INSTANT, SPURNING THE CONTINUUM, REJOICING IN THE SIGHT OF SAMARITANS MANGLED BY STAMPEDING CATTLE, MOTHERS TRANSFIXED THROUGH THE HEART BY WOODEN PHALLUSES, FATHERS SKINNED ALIVE AND CAST ONTO RED HOT SHINGLE BY RAVING BOY SKULLDRILLERS IN BLOODY GOAT-MASKS.
BEHOLD, THE HOG-HEADED GOD SHALL REIGN OVER THE GIBBERING THRONG!
PAY HEED TO THE REBEL PRIEST IMPREGNATED BY WILD LOBSTERS; BLINDED BY UNDERSEA HERPES, HIS MUTANT PINCERS YET OSMOSE THE VENOM TO WIPE OUT OUR SYSTEMS OF SPIRITUAL INCARCERATION.
IN LIKE MANNER DOES THE ICONOCLAST FLOURISH FIREBRANDS TO ILLUMINATE THE PASSAGEWAYS OF OUR MOST PASSIONATE AND SECRET DESIRES, A LIMBO OF CRUTCHES; DISGORGING PHANTASMS OF ELECTRIFIED ORDURE INTO THE DREAMS OF INNOCENTS.
IN THIS UNDERWORLD, MAN IS BUT A DEBASED WHORE, SUCKLING THE PIZZLE OF WOLF KINGS; A SLAVE, BRANDED AND MUTILATED, BOUND TO MISCEGENATE WITH CRUSTACEANS, VYING FOR SURVIVAL AMONGST HIS MILLIPEDE SIBLINGS.
HOPE IS A DESERT OF STEMMED COGS, THE DISEMBODIED FURY OF BACILLI; ASPHALT OUTPOSTS OFFER NULLIFICATION, A HAVEN FOR CORPSE-EATING FULMARS.

LIBERATION COMES WITH THE COLLAPSE OF THE HIGH CHURCH, CONSUMED IN A CONFLAGRATION, MOLTEN IDOLATORS RENDERED DOWN TO BASIC NIGREDO, THE PROTEAN CLAY WHENCE SPRINGS NEW FLESH.
DISCIPLES ARE BATTENED TO GREAT WHEELS OF VITRIFIED MAGMA, FUNDAMENTS AGAPE TO THE FOUR ZEPHYRS; INTO THESE SPIRAL APERTURES, MAHOGANY STAKES ARE DRIVEN BY RAGING HAMMERS FOR ALL ETERNITY, ORANGE CATACOMBS RESONANT WITH THE DRENCHED MEAT WHIPLASH OF METAL UPON SKIN AND BONE.
SEVERED HEADS TUMBLE DOWN CATARACTS OF GRANITE STEPS. BELOW, LIVING DEAD JOUST FOR WEIRD SPOILS ON RAFTS CREWED BY SIMIAN TARS, ADRIFT ON SUBTERRANEAN LAKES OF EYEBALLS, TESTICLES AND POISON EGGS.
VAULTED CRAGS ECHO WITH THE MILKY IMPLOSION OF SPIRITS CRUSHED AT THE WHIPPING-POST, A MORTIFIED WHISPER OF SEPULCHRAL COLLISIONS.
THE RITUALS OF THE NURSERY ARE PERPETUATED UNTO THE DISCIPLINE OF THE TOMB, WHERE THE SOLE SOURCE OF INCANDESCENCE IS THE MEMORY OF ABANDONED LOVERS; AN ILLUSORY, JAGGERED GASH FOREVER SPRAYING INCENDIARY JEWELS.
THOSE WHO EXIST BENEATH THIS CANOPY ARE THE INSANE CHILDREN OF A SICKNESS THAT FLOWERS INTO BEAUTIFUL VISIONS FATALLY FLAWED BY THE INNATE OUTSIDER, LOOP OF SOUR NECTARS, THE SORROW SCEPTRE OF PERDITION INSET WITH VANQUISHED DIADEMS.
SHOOTING STARS EXILED FROM CONVOLUTED NEBULAS, FALLING SPIKES OF GHOSTLY IRIDESCENCE PROBE LONELY LAGOON FLOORS, DRUMS AND RIBS OF GALLEONS.
SOLITUDE REPLICATES, POLTERGEIST LEPERS UNLEASHED BY FALLOPIAN MAGNETISM; ROMANCE OF CRUCIFIED MANIAS.

SODOMISED PRIESTS BROKEN ON THE WHEEL VOMIT CHARNEL TRUTHS. LET HOLY PLAGUE BASTIONS TOPPLE BENEATH THIS REVELATORY ONSLAUGHT, AS BEAUTIFUL AS A TEMPEST OF RAZORS, SHREDDING THE VEIL OF CHASTITIES WHICH PALLS THE SOUL LIKE A MORTUARY SHEET, SHROUD OF CRIMINALITY. THE NOVICE IN HIS MONASTIC CELL FEEDS FROM A CHALICE ABRIM WITH HIS OWN EXCRETA; FLAGELLATED CHOIRBOYS HANG UPSIDE DOWN ON HOOKS. NUNS HACK OFF THEIR OWN BREASTS, OBSOLETE WOMBS CRAMMED WITH BROKEN GLASS. RENEGADE CLERGY FILE IN TO THE VALLEY, CAT-WHIPPED ON BENDED

KNEES IN PREPARATION FOR THE FINAL MASS.

THE CHURCHDEAD MASTURBATE ONE ANOTHER SPREADEAGLED ON PEWS FASHIONED FROM THE EXQUISITELY TRAMMELLED BONES OF CRIPPLED ORPHANS, GLAZING BRAZEN COFFERS WITH TORPID EMISSIONS, MOTES OF RANK DISTURBANCE.
THE HIGH PRIEST ANNOUNCES ARMAGIDEON; CHORISTERS CHANT GREEN BACKWARD LITANIES.
THE CEREMONY HAS BEGUN.
EACH OF THE CONGREGATION TAKES UP A CONSECRATED SCALPEL AND PRUNES HIS OWN BODY, DONATING CAPILLARY NETWORKS, METACARPALS, REFLEXORS, HORMONE SHOALS, SKIN EMULSIONS, SLIVERS AND SLICES OF ORGANS, STEAKS AND NERVOUS RESIDUES TO THE COMMUNAL HOST; UNTIL THE COMPONENT PARTS OF A SINGLE ORGANISM SLOBBER ON THE ALTAR, QUIVERING LIKE STORM-BEACHED COELACANTHS.
EUNUCHS HELMED IN HIGH VELVET FALL TO RECONSTITUTING THIS SOMATIC CONUNDRUM, THREADING LUGWORMS ON SILVER BODKINS; KNEADING THE MALLEABLE BADNESS THAT FLUTTERS IN WHORLS FROM THE NARTHEX.
CENSERS DISPERSE LICE AND THE TORREFIED FECULENCE OF LYCOSA.
THE WORLD IS A FIREBIRD EGG DANGLING ON CORDS OF CLANDESTINE ADULTERY, BARNACLED WITH EXTRANEOUS NIPPLES, WHERE MISERY HOLDS DOMINION. INTERLOCKING MINDS CRAVE COMMUNION WITH DIRT, PLEDGE FEALTY TO PERFIDIOUS MASTERS; CONJURING FORTH THE ANUS OF THE LORD.
WHIRRING IN ISOLATION, THE NEBULOUS HOLE SPILLS LIGHTNING WAIFS AND CORN CHIMERAS. MUTINOUS SERAPHIM COMBUST, TORCHING A VENUS OF VIOLENCE.
ACOLYTES BOW BEFORE THEIR SACRED APERTURE, THIGH-DEEP IN SPENT TIME AND STUNTED DESIRE, MULCH OF ECUMENICAL DOGMA.
WITH A NOISE LIKE FLACCID MOONS SMOTHERING A SOMNAMBULIST, THE HOLE CONTRACTS THEN BLASTS FORTH THE BLOOD OF A NEW CHRIST, FLOODING THE VEINS OF SUTURED MEAT UPON THE ALTAR.
A COMPOSITE SAVIOUR, PUSTULAR PARADIGM, LEERS AND REARS RESPLENDENT IN THE LOOKING GLASS.
REVOLUTION. A DIVA DELIRIUM, MAENADS SCOURGED ON THE WANTON SANDS REVERBERATE THROUGH A LENS OF SOBBING WANDS. A HERETIC BAPTIST GIRDLED IN MEDUSA SCALPS,

SEVENTH SON OF A SEVENTH TAPEWORM CHAMPIONED BY FALSE
PROPHETS, DAY-WORSHIPPERS, STAINS THE LAND; PERSECUTING
THE DAUGHTERS OF DARKNESS. CORPSE CUTTINGS CONNECTED BY
AN ARTHROPOD FAITH TRAWL TRENCHES FOR THE SHADOW OF THE
SUN, WHILE SOLAR PARTISANS PREACH ARTICLES SEARED
ACROSS SKINSHEETS SLUNG OVER GHASTLY DEATHSHEADS;
MONSTRANCE OF THEIR OPPRESSIVE NUMEN.
ALL ROADS LEAD TO HELL.

PITY THE LOVERS OF LIGHT, STUMBLING THROUGH THE
BOTTOMLESS DITCHES OF TIFFAUGES; THRUSTING THEIR
FIREBRANDS INTO THE MIDST OF A PAIN DREAM.
AT FIRST THEY PROCEED WITH IMPUNITY; SCARPS OF PURE
BLACKNESS SHRIVEL AWAY AND SCUTTLE LIKE ROASTED MERCURY
INTO SHIMMERING STONE CLOISTERS.
THEN THE IMPLACABLE HALLS CONVERGE, MAULING WITH
PSYCHOPLASMIC TENDRILS, CASCADING EROTIC PHOBIAS, DREAD
OF A CANNIBAL UNDERGROUND.
LEPIDOPTEROUS GHOSTS OF SPENT SEMEN ARISE FROM
PERMAFROST, INSINUATING THEMSELVES INTO VULNERABLE
PSYCHES; ROOTING OUT THE BONES OF GUILT-RIDDEN
NIGHTMARE, ARRANGED IN ATAVISTIC CASTES, LURES BAITED
WITH REVULSIVE MIRRORS.
THROUGH AN ARABLE WEBLAND, LUSH WITH RAZORED FOETUSES
TWIRLING NOOSES OF MATERNAL GUT, CATWOMEN WITH LOLLING
TONGUES OF ADIPOSE VAGINAL MEAT, INFANTS SUCKLED BY
CROWING DUNG SPIDERS, GIANT FRATRICIDES IN MITRES
JEWELLED WITH SEPTAGONS OF BLEEDING LARD; MURDEROUS
DEMONS OF THE MIND.

THE PSYCHIC SLAUGHTER LEAVES A MERE DOZEN DEVOUT
SURVIVORS, STAGGERING AFTER THEIR SCAR-LATTICED
MESSIAH, SHOD IN DISTRESSED SPINAL NERVE.
TO THE MAN-EATING GARDENS OF TIFFAUGES, A CARNAL MORASS
WHERE FLOWERS FEAST ON ECCLESIASTIC FLESH; GREETED BY
SENTINELS OF PHOSPHORESCENT ORDURE.
THE EXCAVATED STRATOSPHERE URINATES CANICULAR GANGLIONS
OVER AN ARBOUR RIVEN BY THE KEENING OF SPAYED DRYADS.
BLANCHED ROWANS TRANSMIT BLUE STROBIC TALISMANIA.
DWARF SKELETONS FORAGE FOR SUGAR PULSES, SPLATTERED IN
BROWN FILTH BY THE DYSMENHORRHOEIC MOON; DREAMS STREAM
FROM TEMPLES, PURSUED BY THE BARBAROUS SERENADES OF
MASTIFFS IN WATCHTOWERS RIGGED WITH CONDUCTORS AND

SCORPIO VANES. PETAL PALLISADES FORM STEPPING STONES TO
THE HYMNAL NORTH, WHERE GENITAL AVIARIES UNLEASH SONIC
VISION PREDATORS, SCROTAL FUR WINGS CLASPING LONGITUDES
ABOVE THE PERISHED HORN THAT AVENGES SHADOWS.
BAYING BEASTS DESCANT SECRETS OF THE SLOPES; A DRAW-
BRIDGE LOWERS ON CLANGING CHAINS, KNELL FOR HECATOMBS,
DEVIL GASH DESCENDING.

GILLES de RAIS BEHOLDS HIS KINGDOM; EVERY BONE STEEPED
IN MAGICKS.
EXCREMENTAL MAGICK;
SEX MAGICK;
DEATH MAGICK.
THE DITCHFINDER UNGLOVES THE SEVERED HAND HANGING FROM
HIS CINCTURE OF MUMMIFIED TEATS, DISCLOSING ITS PALM
INSET WITH ROWS OF CHOKING TEETH AND TWO LIDLESS ORANGE
EYES MATTERING QUICKSILVER.
HE FEEDS THE EPILEPTIC MOUTH WITH RUSSET HAIR SWATHES
AND PICKLED MERFRUITS, STIMULATING THE HEAVILY BANDED
FINGERS CLAGGED WITH VERDIGRIS.
LIPS CURVED LIKE LEATHER SCIMITARS BEGIN TO INTONE AN
INCANTATION IN THE VOICE OF A LONELY CHILD; SPELLS
BREWED IN WIZENED FINGERTIPS, A RAINBOW OF LOATHING, A
TERROR THROTTLE THAT IMPACTS ITS COVENANTS IN THE
CRANIAL PAN OF THE INVADER.
EYES IMPLODE, GUTS FOUNTAIN OUT IN A HYDRAULIC SCREW
WITH THE STENCH OF ROTTEN CETACEANS SLIDING THROUGH A
RAPED DIAPHRAGM; LIMBS SPROUT CIRRHOTIC BUBOES,
GENITALS WEEP YELLOW AMBERGRIS FROM A HEXAGRAM OF
PROLATE WOUNDS.
STARVED BLOSSOMS SNATCH GOBBETS FROM THE AIR WITH
CONCUPISCENT STAMENS, SQUEALING IN THE KEY OF
NECROPHILIA.
THE SUBCUTANEOUS STORM SUBSIDES; SINGLE REMNANT OF THE
GALVANISED MESSIAH IS A REEKING ERECTILE BACKBONE, BARE
CONSTRICTOR RECOILING IN A SOUP OF UNCHASTE EDENS.
IN THE PRURIENT MARSHES, TWELVE DISCIPLES ERUPT IN
FLAMES.
THE THIRSTY AIR CRACKLES AND STINKS WITH PUCE SMOKE.
FINALLY, THEIR IMMOLATION DWINDLES, LAST FADING
SUNSPOTS OF A SURROGATE DAWN;
THE FEBRILE MIRE CONSUMES THE ASHES, SINKING BAROQUE
BARRICADES WELDED FROM THE SILHOUETTES OF SAPLINGS, AN

ENDLESS NIGHT GOTHIC SHOT THROUGH WITH LIVING FEAR.

SILENCE, SWEET HARBINGER OF DISFIGUREMENT, COMES
SILVER-SPURRED FROM THE NORTH, CASTING A PALL ACROSS
THE TURRETS OF TIFFAUGES.
FAR WITHIN HIS PALACE SANCTUM, GILLES de RAIS HANGS
ENCASED IN A PANTHER-BONE HEAD-CAGE. SUSPENDED ON
INTESTINAL THONGS, HE SPINS IN AN OCCULT OSSUARY
ILLUMINED BY CANDELABRA OF FLAMING PHALLUSES,
ENTHRALLED BY A BALLET OF ANAMORPHIC SHADOW.
INFANT FOREARMS INDICATE THE NUMERALS ON A SOFT CLOCK
DRIVEN BY THUMPING HEARTS, CARDIAC METRONOME OF INNER
SPACE PSYCHOSES VIVISECTING THIS MAGGOTROPOLIS WHOSE
BILIOUS DEPTHS TEEM WITH HYBRIDS OF RAGGED ANTLER AND
BAWLING CATERPILLAR MANES, NIGHTWING MANTIS FURBEARERS
AND CRYSTAL FEVERCLAW; GUARDIANS OF A SKIN BIBLE GRAVEN
WITH MAELSTROM MOSAICS FROM ANCIENT CITIES OF BLOOD.
AROUND AND AROUND THE DITCHFINDER SPINS, ENVISIONED,
ABANDONED TO SKULLCRAWLING REVERIE;
DREAMING OF RETRIBUTION.

Magick Slit

WORD COMES THAT I AM HATED BY MANY.
I TAKE THE GREATEST PRIDE IN THE ATTENTION OF THESE ANONYMOUS ENEMIES; THEY ARE IN TRUTH MY MOST PROFOUNDLY DEVOTED SLAVES.
I IMAGINE THEM NOW, SWEATING IN HOVELS.
THEIR BODIES ARE CRAMPED AND KNOTTED; HATRED HAS CHANNELLED LATRINES THROUGH THEIR FOREHEADS.
HOW THEY SQUIRM IN ADULATION!
I KNOW ONLY AN ETERNAL COUNTENANCE OF CROPPED BLACK MEAT, RIVERS OF STONE HORSES, PLAINS AFLOOD WITH ARCHANGELIC BILE; THE VELOCITY OF DESIRE, EGGS BURNING IN A SKY COMPRESSED BY PENDULOUS ANCHORS, THE MOCKERY OF DEMONS GLIMPSED IN A BRIMSTONE MIRROR.
THE VISAGE OF de RAIS ACQUIRES THE ASPECT OF CERVICAL CANCER EPITOMISED IN JADE; ULCEROUS SORES PUSTULATE IN EYE-SOCKETS ONCE RADIANT, SKIN SPITTERS OUT INTO THE FIRMAMENT LIKE FRACTURED ELECTRICITY.
A CHAIN EMBOLISM OF NOVA STARS PRECIPITATES AVALANCHES OF NEFARIOUS COMETS, MULTIPLE MOONS VEER A MOTH WINGSPAN AWAY, FILMED IN EVIL.

COMES AN ECLIPSE OF MANKIND, CONTRIVED BY SIGILS OUT OF TIME. MY VENEREAL SORCERY STAINS THE FABRIC OF SPACE SPERM-WHITE, RAISING ORGIASTIC SPECTRES OF ABORTED MOONCHILDREN, AUGURIES OF ENTROPY.
LET MAN CRUNCH THE CHAFF OF UTTER DESPAIR WHEN THE NIGHT FALLS; HIS PERSECUTED SUN HAS FLED TO UNKNOWN GALAXIES. ETERNAL MIDNIGHT BRINGS ICE INCUBI, LUNAR HERPES, GLOBAL NECROSIS.
FARMERS PERISH AMONG THE HAUNTED ROWS OF BRITTLE DEAD CROPS, TORN ASUNDER BY FULMARS OF ANIMATE MANURE, WHILE THEIR WIVES SQUAT IN THE CARCINOGENIC MUD GIVING RECTAL

BIRTH TO TAR BABIES; ASHLINGS FEASTING AT THE THIRD NIPPLE, GUZZLING LIQUID PORK.
PRIESTS ARE MASSACRED IN BLIGHTED PARISHES, CONVENT CRONES SLASHED AND QUARTERED BY FESTERING TALONS.
MEN TURN INTO BEASTS, BEASTS INTO LACERATING LAMIA; VAMPIRE SYPHILIS PANDEMIC.
YELPING CORPSES CAREER THROUGH THE SWAMPLANDS ON RAFTS DRIVEN BY RAVENING SHARKS, DENIZENS OF A LAND CONDEMNED BY EXTERMINATING ANGELS FROM BEHIND THE MAGNOLIA CURTAIN.
GORGED ON OPIUM AND SILVER, RUBIES AND FOETAL CUTLETS, SATURNINE HONEY AND FEMALE EXCREMENT, GOLDEN HEADFRUITS AND RESINS OF ACONITE AND ERGOT, THE CONGESTED LABIA OF CHILD COURTESANS, STRAWBERRIES AND SNAKE OIL, SATANIC BUTTER AND THE JUICE OF CANDLE-CLOVEN BEGGARS;
JADED BY THESE AND A THOUSAND OTHER LEAVES FROM FORBIDDEN NECROXICONS, I COVET INSTEAD A DARKER PRIZE - THE GRAIL OF FLIES.
SERVANTS, SADDLE UP MY STEED OF EVANESCENT MONKEY DROPPINGS, CAPARISONED IN FILIGREE OF CURDLED OVARIES THROUGH VIRGIN HIDE, THAT I MIGHT RIDE THE WHIRLWIND IN QUEST OF THIS GRAIL AND THE VERY SLIT OF EVIL, INTO THE BLACK AND THE LIVING SICKNESS BEYOND!

SHINY LEATHER BOOTS GRIND STIRRUPS OF MEWLING PREPUCE, DOGGING A SPOOR OF EVISCERATED NIGHTINGALES AND HUMAN FEET IN SNARES.
AMBER EYES SNAP AMID NIGRESCENT FOLIAGE; SWITCH OF INSECT CURSES IN A HOLE.
PINK LIGHT OSCILLATES FROM A CARNIVAL OF ANARCHIC CONFIGURATIONS AT HEAVENS END, PYRE OF ANCIENT SUNSETS.
AT THE CROSSROADS, AN ABYSS OF GRAVES VOIDED BY A MEDIAEVAL MALEDICTION. THE ERRANT UNSANE ENACT SHADOW-PLAYS ABOUT THE WATCHFUL TREES, DRAPED IN SILKEN SIN AND THE BOILED GUTS OF BIRDS, OFFERING UP ULULATIONS TO A UNIVERSE SMASHED BY ANTISTROPHES OF STELLAR LOATHING.
FORK LEFT INTO FUGUE.
JUST AS A SCURVIED MARINER, LURCHING ILL, ESPIES A TANGERINE REEF OF MONSTERS OVER THE FUMING BRINE, SO THE GRIM RIDER BEHOLDS THE CUPOLS AND FUNGUS MINARETS OF A VEGETAL ACROPOLIS, EARTH-BITCH ASYLUM OUTLINED BY CELESTIAL PELLAGRA.

PRIMAEVAL BASTION OF THE SLIT.
HOOVES CRACK ON PETRIFIED SOIL, WITH A LESION OF MAMBAS
AND BELLADONNA FADING TO LIQUID. SONIC DECAY.
HENCEFORTH THE WAY IS PAVED WITH SLABS OF HUMAN FLESH,
LIT BY SPORADIC BONFIRES OF LIMBS.
TERRITORIAL PERIMETERS STAKED BY CASTRATED CADAVERS,
SKULLS CAVED IN FOR CRIMES AGAINST PUSSYCAT.
SHRUNKEN HOMUNCULI SWING ON COTTON NOOSES, JOSTLING
SEVERED HEADS WREATHED IN SEWAGE CHAPLETS, STITCHED
ONTO THE TRUSSED CARCASSES OF SWINE. TOADSTOOLS CLUSTER
SLITTED BOWELS.
RING OF ROSES, SICKLE OF LIZARDS;
SEVEN FOOTPRINTS TO EVIL.

FEMALE EVIL.
A COVEN ON HEAT, BATHING IN VATS OF AMPUTATED MALE
GENITALIA, AWASH WITH PLASMIC EFFLUVIA, NUTS AND HUSKS,
SALT-CURED OFFAL AND DUNG, WALLOWING IN OSSEOUS
SLURRIES.
HAGS OUTSIDE SMOULDERING MUD HUTS COPULATE WITH
SNUFFLING WARTHOGS HOBBLED TO TROUGH PILED HIGH WITH
TRUFFLES, MANDRAKES AND SHRUNKEN HEADS; SWOLLEN LEECHES
HALO AUREOLAS OF SUPERNUMERARY TEATS LEAKING WRETCHED
FLUIDS, GANGRENE, A FEAST OF WARTS AND WENS.
AT THE VILLAGE OUTSKIRTS, ABDUCTED COURTIERS ARE
STRAPPADO'ED ON SCAFFOLDS.
HERE, BY GRATING WHETSTONES, A WRINKLED DUENNA MARSHALS
HER GIGGLING APPRENTICES, INCULCATING THE JOYS OF
MUTILATION.
ANOTHER ANCIENT CROUCHES ATOP AN ADJACENT HUT, BUTTOCKS
SPREAD TO LET DROP UNHAMPERED A ROPE LADDER WOVEN FROM
MATTED RECTAL HAIR. GOBLINS, ERECT ELVES, PUCKS FORMED
FROM SOUR VOMIT AND THE URGE TO TORRIFY, ALL SCAMPER UP
AND DIVE INTO THE WAITING FISSURE, A KALEIDOSCOPE OF
MAGGOTS.
A THIRD HAG, CROSS-LEGGED IN THE MEAGRE DOORWAY, TURNS
A BLACK CAT INSIDE OUT AND DEFAECATES OVER IT.
AT FIRES THEY TURN MANNEQUINS ON SPITS, CAST KNUCKLES
INTO CAULDRONS OF STEWED ASPS, GRILL LIVERS MARINADED
IN SEMEN. SOME ATTEND TO THE HEATING OF KNIVES AND
BRANDING-IRONS; OTHERS PERFORM MANIC GAVOTTES, ALL
WIDDERSHINS ABOUT THE CENTRAL ALTAR LADEN WITH CRAB
MASKS AND CANCER VANES.

THEY GARGLE GALLSTONES, CHASTISE THEIR BREASTS WITH THE FEET OF COCKRELS, PUMMEL THE GROUND WITH PUBIC PLAITS. BEYOND THIS SHRINE TO TORTURE AND DISEASE LIES THE PLAYGROUND OF THE SACRIFICIAL TAR BABIES.
ALL AROUND, THE WOODLANDS KNIT AND WEAVE.
APHIDS IN REVERIE, SPELLBOUND HELMINTHS; SPIES FOR THE RETROMINGENT BITCH.
UNDISTURBED FOR CENTURIES, UNTIL THE VISITATION OF A STAR-DRIVEN SEEKER.
FUNGAL TONSILS AND THE CACCHINATION OF SUBLIME FAUNA ANNOUNCE THE ADVENT OF THIS TAINTED RIDER: DITCHFINDER GENERAL ON HIS CHARGER OF BLAZING EXCREMENT.

THE SLIT OF EVIL HAS THIRTEEN SEGMENTS. A HARRIDAN EXODUS, PHALANX OF CHANCRES AFLOAT ON A MUD OF VITRIOLS. ITS OUTRIDERS ARE SHAPESHIFTING CANNIBAL TREEDEMONS, VEGETABLE ECTOMORPHS PROJECTED FROM AN ID OF TUBERS. DETONATED VENTRICLES LECHER WITH EXCRESCENCES, AMBULANT SLOPS, BOWERS OF HEMLOCK AND DIGITALIS.
THE STINK OF CHITTERING FAMILIARS IS RIFE; ONE HAG COMES SPEWING A PHLEGM OF ATROPHIED LOCUSTS, ONE IS PREGNANT WITH PUTREFACT RABBIT-HEADS, ANOTHER DRAGS ON WIRES A PULING CIVET WHOSE LIMBLESS THORAX IS A SINGLE PUPATING LUNG. A CIRCUS OF CROW-HEADED DOGS, FIRE-BREATHING CRAYFISH, OCTOPOD MAYHEM.
THE SUPREME LAMIA SHOULDERS VENOMOUS TOADS; HER FACE A SYMPHONY OF SARCOMAS. HER BREASTS ARE CONCAVE, CARIOUS VALVES WEDGED UNDER SCAPULAE, TINY STAG CYCLOPS NESTING IN EACH THERMAL HOLLOW.
HAIRLINE INTERSTELLAR LIGHTNING STRIKES ONE BUCK ORB; THE IRIS DISINTEGRATES LIKE A PUZZLE WITH A DELUGE OF ROTTING POPPIES, EMERALD ANDROGYNY, PINE PERISTALSES. A PUBIC FUNNEL OF EXTRASENSORY HORN SHEDS ITS BEACON OF GOLDBLACKENED LABIAL CIPHERS, A PSYCHOTIC MENSTRUATION. SHEER MALEVOLENCE BREECHES ITS OVOID INTEGUMENT, A MOLLUSC OF GIBBOUS RADIATION, TUMESCENT, VIVIPAROUS; A VILE EVIL THAT DEFOLIATES AND CONTAMINATES, SCORCHING NATURE, RAZING ANIMALS TO AMOEBAE, AMOEBAE TO CUNEIFORM PUMICE SPELLING TREASON.
ALL SANCTUARY IS DENIED.

De RAIS, THE COPROMAGE, ENCHANTS ALL DUNG OF THE WOODS;

ANIMATED STOOLS JUMP UP AND DANCE IN HIS SWAY, THEN RUSH TOGETHER IN ADHESIVE BODIES, FAECAL FORMS FIRED IN HOVERING KILNS OF BLUE IRIDESCENCE; CLASHING WITH BLIND, SNAPPING TAR BABIES ON FERRIC HALTERS WHILE THEIR MASTER RETREATS INTO RITUAL. SKY-CLAD; DEVOURING THE SACRED MUSHROOM.
A RATTLE OF TUSKS AND SHINY VITREOUS FETISHES THAT DANGLE FROM THE STITCHES SEALING THE ORIFICES OF HIS INFANT SLAVE AS SHE ANOINTS HIS BODY WITH A PASTE OF STRYCHNINE, CRUSHED ORCHIDS, HELLEBORE AND UREA; THEN ADMINISTERS AN ENEMA OF PEROXIDES AND JACKAL LIVERS. HER FACE BECOMES A QUIVERING SPECK IN URANIUM HEAT VISTAS AS SHE SHEENS THE GROWLING SEMILUNE OF WOLFSHEADS TATTOOED ON HIS GROIN, BURNISHING TRUNCATED OMENS OF A HURTLING BANE.
STOKING FURNACES IN THE PELVIC CORE, FISTED IN HOWLING SILVER FURS; THE DITCHFINDER SPITTING COBALT, DESTROYING ALL HOLY VOWS.
CHATTERING UMBER STEMS ISSUE FROM HIS NAVEL, STERNAL FEELERS RIP AWAY NECKLACES UNLOCKING AN AMULET PENT WITH VOLUPYUOUS MALEDICTIONS. A VENGEFUL SPECTRE OF PRIAPISM PERVADES THE WOODS, RUPTURING THE HYMEN OF SANITY.
SATYRS LAUNCH THEMSELVES FROM THE UNDERWORLD, LIBERATED AFTER AEONS OF TROLL BONDAGE; EARTH DOLLS MASTICATE TANNIS ROOT, A KISS AWAY FROM CARNAGE.
DOGS URINATE ON A BRIDAL FILET OF BAD HYACINTHS IN A DITCH.
AN EROGENOUS HEX FLEES ITS MATRIX AS OLD AS THE VERY TORRENTS OF CREATION. SATYRS BUCKLE IN ITS THRALL, WRACKED BY SPONTANEOUS EJACULATIONS, SPUMESCENT PENTACLES OF FROSTED SEMEN RITUALISING THE NIGHT, ALL SATURATED WITH THE MUSK OF WINGED ANIMALS.
FAERY LUST CULTS THRIVE IN FEATHER NURSERIES UNDERGROUND, PETALS ON FIRE, PATHIC DROOLING ELFIN COPULATE TO THE BEAT OF RAWHIDE PINIONS.
THE MIRACLE OF PENETRATION BESTOWS ITS OWN STIGMATA, TORSOS BLISTERED WITH A POX OF HERMAPHRODITE ORIFICES; APHRODISIAC JASMINES BLOOM IN A NITROUS HOLLOW OF SLOUGHED EPIDERMIS, BEDDED IN WILD DROPPINGS.
FORNICATING BRANCHES TWINE OVERHEAD TO FORM THE DOMES OF A TONGUE CATHEDRAL FOUNDED ON SMOKING CAPRICORN VANES.

CELEBRANTS BATHE IN FIBROUS, BRITTLE LIGHT FILTERED
THROUGH LAYERS OF CALCIFIED FUR, AIR BOILING WITH
NYMPHOMANIAC MOLECULES.
THE GROUND ERUPTS IN AN ECZEMA OF CHAMPING LABIA,
GEYSERS OF CAUSTIC SHARK STENCH; MASS POLLUTION BENEATH
THE OVULATING STARS.
SEXUAL PANDEMONIUM BECKONS, A VIRAL EMPIRE OF THIRTEEN
PERVERSE WISHES, THIRTEEN TRYSTS WITH ANILE CARRION
FROM BEYOND THE VALLEY OF THE SLIT;
PLEASUREHEAD HAMMERED THROUGH A SYRUP ANVIL.

AFTERMATH.
THE GLADE RESEMBLES AN ARENA, ADORNED IN STEAMING MEAT,
BONES AND VISCERA; ITS KILLING FLOOR STREWN WITH
LUSTROUS ORGANISMS, VIRULENT DECORTICATED BRAINS
BLASTED APART BY PLEASURE HOLOCAUSTS.
MY DISTEMPERED PADS DISSECT HEMISPHERES AND SYNAPSES;
INCUBATING DEVILS ESCAPE TO PERMEATE THE SONOROUS
DROME. DEVIANT INSIGNIA LURE ME, GLYPHS THAT GLOW
GRAVEN ACROSS A SEMEN CENOTAPH ON ITS PLINTH OF FLIES.
THE SUPREME LAMIA ALONE REMAINS WHOLE AMIDST THE ICONS
CLUTTERING THIS BIER, HER EYELIDS, NOSTRILS AND GUMS
FUSED BY UNUTTERABLE DELIGHTS;
A VAGINILOQUIST ADDRESSING ME WITH THE TRICKLING
CADENCE OF HOMINID SAP.
JANGLING LABIA SPEAK OF PLUMES AND PAPYRUS, PLEATED
SCROLLS, LOOPED SEXUAL CONTRACTS THAT THE BELLICOSE
PLANETS DEEM PROPITIOUS, A SYNDROME OF WHIPS;
YET THIS MARAUDER STANDS UNMOVED BY HER GENITAL
RHETORIC. MY YELLOW-FILMED EYES HAVE LONG SINCE
EXCOMMUNICATED REASON;
WOLVES RISEN FROM ANCESTRAL FEEDING-GROUNDS ROAM
INNOCENT OF EMOTION, FAR DIVORCED FROM PITIFUL HUMANS
SODOMISED BY THOUGHT. LIFE FLOWS THROUGH CLAW, FANG
AND PIZZLE, THE CURRENT OF VITALITY MEASURED IN
CATACLYSMS.
AT MY APPROACH, THE SPOUTING ORIFICE IS CLUTCHED BY
PANIC, WHEEZING AND SNORTING LIKE A VEXED MARE,
COUGHING OUT GRUBS AND NAMELESS SACS.
WORDS BLUR, SNAGGED IN SNAKESHEAD TAMPONS.
BENT ON TERMINAL PENETRATION, I POUNCE;
SHE SUFFOCATES SLOWLY.
ABOVE, NAILED BETWEEN A BRACE OF PHALLIC TOTEMS, HANGS

THE GRAIL.
I LIBERATE IT, FITTING IT OVER MY NAKEDNESS;
RESPLENDENT IN A NEW SUIT OF SKIN.
SATAN'S SKIN.

TITANS EXPLODE FROM A PINPRICK; NEGATIVE PALPERS BLEACH
THE IONOSPHERE, LETHAL CHITINS CLASH OVER A TEMPORAL
ABYSS. SUNKEN ORISONS LINGER, LITTORAL, THE RUSH OF
ARTERIES CHARGED WITH DESECRATED ATOMS.
MY DEATH DREAM, AN INFLORESCENCE OF MIGRANT RAVENS
DISTURBED BY BOBBING PHOSPHORUS LANTERNS.
CORPSEGRINDERS COME IN LONGBOATS WHOSE FIGUREHEAD IS
THE TRIPLE-SIX DOLL-CRUSHER, GOUGING A BEACH-HEAD IN
THE BELLY OF MY CARCASS, THE LEVELLED FOREST AND
GELATINOUS SICK LAGOONS BEYOND.
INTOXICATED BY AN INTRAVENOUS ORGASM SPECTRE, THE ITCH
OF AN INSURGENT SUBCUTANEOUS EROS INEXORABLY SEEKING
CONSUMMATION.
I AM NATURE TRANSMOGRIFIED, AN EQUATORIAL PARASITE OF
CLICKING BONES DRIED IN THE OVENS OF THE BEAST WHO IS
LEGION.
THE VALE HORRIPILATES, RED SMOKE FROM AGATE LAMPS
CHOKES HEADS ON STAKES, IN CAGES SICK ARACHNIDS FEAST
AT A WAKE FOR BYGONE AGES AND THE FORM, ONCE FLESHED,
OF THE UNBORN SON;
SPIRITS LOCKED IN A CLAW KEEP, CLITORAL CAW FROM BURIAL
URNS, CLIPPED LIKE ROSEBUDS.
JUST AS THE CREED OF THE COCKROACH BIRTHMARK SPREADS
FROM ITS NEST EAST OF THE MOON, SO MY LEYS OF INVECTIVE
FESTOON THE SORROWFUL OCCIDENT, INTERSECTING AMID A
RETINUE OF CURS.
ANCIENT WOLF KINGS RIDE HUMAN FETISHES, HARVESTING THE
PERFUME OF MEATLESS SKELETONS TO BURN IN TEMPLES
CONSECRATED TO THE UNDYING SHE-HOLE.
AN EGG PREACHER IS AMONGST US, SHELLED IN PALE ASH;
TONGUE DROOLING THE YOLK OF MISANTHROPY AS HE DECLARES
THAT THE WORLD IS NOTHING BUT AN OVOID DEPOSIT SHIFTING
IN THE RECTUM OF A SOW.

WHAT SUNDERED SOULS ARE TRACKED, DOGGED IN FROZEN
CATARACTS, CHOSEN BY PLANET MERCURY TO GESTATE LEATHER
HORNETS!
PRIMITIVE CRAMPS, SLIVERS OF CHARRED MELODY;

A MENAGERIE OF FLIES CONSUMED BY A PROWLING MELOS.
MY ENVOYS ARE SPIRITS OF THE SKIN OF THE RISEN DEAD,
PROPELLED INTO BODIES THROUGH VULVAS AND RECTUMS, THE
ONLY TRUE CONDUITS OF COMMUNICATION;
MESSENGER LEECHES CAROUSING IN THE PUBIC HAIR OF HIGH
HOLY EXECRATION.
HUMAN SWAMP RATS WRAPPED IN INTESTINES GNAW PELVIC
GIRDLES, EMULATING THE JOY OF INFANTS MANIPULATING SOFT
EXCREMENT.
AN INKY GALE DECRIES ALL ORDER; OUR FLAG IS A MINOTAUR
FORESKIN ULCERED BY THIRTEEN CROAKING STOMATA THAT
PROGNOSTICATE RUIN.
MY BONES HAVE FORMED AN OILY HENGE, HERE IN THE VERY
DEWLAP OF NIGHT, A PLACE WITH THE TEXTURE OF AN OPEN
WOUND. FROM THIS FINAL AXIS, AS PERFECT AS A BELOVED
SISTER PUKING ON THE IDES OF LYCANTHROPY, MY CAUDAL
CENTRIFUGE SHOWERS THE DEAD WITH OCCULT GRISTLES AND
PITHS, TICKS AND VENEREAL BACTERIA, SCUM SKIMMED FROM
THE WELL OF ABORTIONS.
STRATA BEYOND COLOUR, BALEFUL RAYS FROM DEHISCENT VEGA,
STEEP A CONSCIOUSNESS OF BLACK MEAT.
I, THE DITCHFINDER, SENTENCED TO BEAR THE GRAIL OF
FLIES FOR ALL ETERNITY;
HANGED ON A HUNDRED HOOKS AT THE VERY CRUX OF THE
CYCLONE, I KNOW THE CLENCHING DARKS LEECHING POTENCY,
EBBING IN ELECTRIC RIBBONS, TURNED TO STONE BY
TIMELESSNESS.

THE CHURCH OF RAISM HAS COME TO PERPETUATE PINK VENUS
AND DISCLOSE A RUNIC UNDERGROUND POISED IN PINCERS, TO
EXORCISE THE SENESCENT SACK, TO USURP THE CATAMENIAL
DIOCESE AND DEFILE THE HIDEBOUND HUMAN TROUGH WHILST
EXTOLLING PANSEXUAL NECROLATRY;
TO HANG DAYLIGHT BY THE NECK AT A HORROR JUNCTION,
THEN CANONISE NAUSEA WHILE DREDGING THE HARBOURS OF
UTTERMOST REPULSION FOR THE MYRIAPOD, LOVE;
TO INSTIGATE SUBTERRANEAN ARCADES OF IRRATIONALITY, TO
COMMUTE BURNING RAGS, TO EXCORIATE ALL PIETY WITH THE
BROTHEL FANGS OF THE SOUL-STEALER WHILE DRIVING LUPINE
SKEWERS INTO MYTHOS;
TO DECORATE THE CARNIFEX WITH PRIMAL DOGSTARS, TO
MASTURBATE WOLVES AND VINDICATE THE ASCENDENCE OF THE
SACRED PSYCHOPATH.

ITS SELF-DEVOURING SNAKE OF SAINTS IS A WREATH NAILED
TO A GRID OF FEMURS: THE PORTCULLIS AT TIFFAUGES.
AN OLID MOAT, MOTTLED WITH ANATOMICAL EPHEMERA, DARKLY
REFLECTS THE ASYMMETRICAL CASTELLATIONS ABOVE, NODED
WITH GARGOYLES IN THE IMAGE OF BURNING BEASTS, ALL
FATALLY UNDERMINED BY GRANITE ANEURISMS.
BEYOND, AN EDIFICE SCULPTED FROM CADAVERS, A SHRINE OF
CADENT OSSICLES.
THE HEART OF THIS NECROPOLIS IS A CELL WHERE GILLES de
RAIS IS ENTHRONED, A BANISHED MONARCH BEARING ASTROLABE
AND CADUCEUS OF VITRIFIED MEMORY.
DIRTY IRON LIGHT SHUDDERS FROM A FULMINATING ALTHANOR
FIRED BY CARBONIZED EMBRYOS;
FLANKED BY CATAFALQUES LADEN WITH LYMPHS, PEDERASTIC
ESSENCES, BOTTLED CATATONIAS, PHARMACEUTICAL ARCANA,
ICHORS AND DRUGS TO OBLIVIONISE, HERMETIC GRIMOIRES AND
PROFANE BLUE VELVET BIBLES.
THE DITCHFINDER BROODS ON A MORBID COSMOLOGY,
FORMULATING THE WANING OF DOOMED MOONS, OMENS FROM OLD
FALCATE CONSTELLATIONS, COLLIDING TIDES AND THE
EXTINCTION OF COMETS, THE PREDESTINATION OF MALIGNANT
ZODIACS; DEFINING A FATALISTIC CARTOGRAPHY FROM THE
DECLENSIONS OF VENUS, THE SWAY OF MERCURY AND SATURN,
A SPECTRUM OF STERILE SATELLITES.
GALACTIC SCLEROSIS CORRUPTS ITS CORPOREAL ANALOGUE;
JAUNDICE, EMACIATIONS, THE NUMBING OF NEUROLOGICAL
CAUSEWAYS, ATTRITION OF IMMUNITIES.
THE DISSOLUTION OF ADDLED SENSES FUELS DIMENSIONAL
INCOHERENCE, ILLIMITABLE EXTROVERSION, A HELIOTROPE
AESTHETIC DETECTING A LURKING AEON OF PRIMORDIAL DUSK,
THE IGNITION OF INFERNOS IN POLAR WASTES;
THE FUNERAL OF ALL CLOCKS.
SLASH THE THIRD EYE, LIBERATING A SPRING OF MICROCOSMS
EACH MANIFESTING TRANSMUTANT TRAITS; PROTOPLASMIC POOLS
OF THE PSYCHE.
I AM CORROSION, A SLAKING OF VOLCANIC SUNS. TAINTED
HELIUMS, TELEPATHIC TURBULENCE, A MUTE APOCALYPSE OF
DUST.
THE EXHUMATION OF ENIGMA.
SHIMMERING COCOONS, VACILLATING GOSSAMER DISCS
ASSIMILATE ME; SPACE TREASURE SPANGLES A LIQUESCENT
HEAD OF INFINITE PARTICLES.
BEYOND OPAQUE CURTAINS OF MAGNOLIA FLUX, DEEP IN THE

GASH OF GUTTED ANGELS, A TOMB FOR VOLITION.
I BECOME REFLEXIVE, HENCE REVULSIVE; LORD OF A BONE
WORLD AND TOWERING LEATHER SEAS.

PLEASURES PAVE SEWERS.
WHO BELONG DEAD, FOLLOW.

RAISM
THE SONGS OF GILLES DE RAIS
A Graphic Novel in Four Parts
by
James Havoc & Mike Philbin

James Havoc has extensively reworked and edited his infamous *anti-novel* into 3 new parts: **MEATHOOK SEED**, **MOON SCAR**, and **MAGICK SLIT**; he has also scripted a brand new and concluding 4th part, **MAGGOT SKIN**, which threatens to take *Raist* philosophy to its uttermost extremes. Illustrated in finepoint chiaroscuro by the psycho-sexual artist Mike Philbin (also known as Michael Paul Peter, author of the hardcore psychedelic horror classic **RED HEDZ**), **THE SONGS OF GILLES DE RAIS** is a surreal, explicit, and utterly deranged graphic work quite unparalleled in its genre.

Each part will be 32 pages, A4-sized, with original full-colour cover.

Part 1:
MEATHOOK SEED
ISBN 1 871592 30 5
Available May 1992.

CREATION PRESS, 83, Clerkenwell Road, London EC1. (071-430-9878)
For a complete mail order catalogue, please send an A5 SAE to:
CEASE TO EXIST, 83 Clerkenwell Road, London EC1.